THE SPIDER:
CITY OF DREADFUL NIGHT

MASTER OF MEN!

THE SPIDER ®

CITY OF
DREADFUL NIGHT

By Grant Stockbridge

STEEGER BOOKS • 2020

CHAPTER 1
"THE SPIDER IS DOOMED!"

IN THE Borough of Queens, in the City of New York, there is a small, private airplane landing field that is not charted on any Department of Commerce maps. This field is located not far from Newtown Creek, and to the casual eye of the passerby it appears to be nothing more than the well-kept lawn of some wealthy estate, surrounded by a carefully trimmed hedge.

Toward this landing field, a black, low winged monoplane angled down from the west, mooring like a black wraith, practically invisible in the night. The pilot had shut off his motor at five hundred feet, and he crossed the hedge noiselessly, without attracting the attention of the patrolman on the beat two blocks away. Simultaneously with the arrival of the monoplane over the hedge, low ground beacons came to light on the field, laying a dully glowing path of light for the pilot's landing. Those beacons had been brought to life by the interruption of a photo-electric ray which ran along the entire length of the hedge.

In less than a minute the plane had rolled to a perfect landing, and the beacons clicked off.

Richard Wentworth climbed out of the cockpit, and rolled the tight plane into a low shed which might have been a gardener's cottage, but which was really a combination garage and hangar. The doors of the shed were opened by photoelectric rays, and closed automatically once the machine was inside.

1

Wentworth did not turn on any light. Instead, he felt around the wall in the darkness until he reached one of the four windows, each set in one of the walls. He pulled up the heavy leather shade, and peered out toward the west. There was a heavy fog over the East River, but he could make out the lights of Manhattan, and the gray bulk of the Williamsburg Bridge. Criss-crossed above Manhattan Island were dozens of fingering searchlights, poking into the air. And from the river came the dim squeal of fog-horns and the screech of sirens on police launches.

In the darkness, Richard Wentworth's sensitive mouth tightened into a grim line, and a strange fire leaped into his

Tang-akhmut was intoning: "So ye shall obey me to the letter."

eyes. Those questing searchlights, those foghorns and those sirens were all for him. Manhattan was full of peril for man tonight. As Richard Wentworth, the police wanted him for murder—a murder he had not committed, but one which had been cunningly placed at his door. As the Spider, both the police and the underworld would show him short shrift.

The Spider, whose guns had blasted death at so many vicious criminals, was himself proscribed by the law. There was not a policeman in all New York tonight who would not give an arm for the privilege of capturing or killing the Spider. And the underworld hated him with a hot, unforgiving hatred.

Tang-akhmut, that sinister Man from the East, had planned well—so well, that now, two weeks after Wentworth had heard the Man's dying screams, Wentworth himself did not dare to enter New York openly. He had flown toward Mitchell Field, but the sight of those searchlights had warned him off. There were few places where he could go now, for the Man from the East had waged a bitter, merciless war against him from the very start, stripping him of all his wealth, and all the resources he had made use of in his continuous battle against crime. Wentworth had for a moment known panic when he understood that he could not enter New York by any ordinary means. And then, while still in the air, he had thought of this little landing field, which he had long ago purchased in the name of a young lady— his fiancée, in fact.

In searching out and depriving him of every last possession of his own, he wondered if Tang-akhmut had overlooked this field, not registered in his own name. So he had taken the chance;

and so far, it seemed that fortune smiled on him—for he had landed unmolested.

There was much to be done in New York—and much peril to be braved. Word had come to him, in the West, that New York seemed to be in the grip of as evil a force as Tang-akhmut had ever been. High officials were subservient to some unknown power that committed crime after crime, depredation after depredation, without interference from the police or from any other duly constituted authority. The only explanation for this was that some of Tang-akhmut's henchmen had taken over the organization which that man of evil had built up here. And Wentworth saw it as his duty to smash the last remnants of that organization before, Phoenix-like, they rose from the ashes.

He peered to the west at the searching lights, and sighed. They wanted the Spider more than they wanted Wentworth. But it was as the Spider that he must enter the city tonight. There was a telephone at the other end of the building, and he pulled down the shade, started to turn, to make his way toward it Abruptly he stopped in the pitch blackness, his nerves tingling, his ears cocked for a repetition of the breath of movement that had come to him from somewhere in the blackness to his left.

INSTINCTIVELY HE crouched, and a small swishing noise whirred above his head. His hand went up automatically, caught at the thin strand of looped wire that had been cast at him. Fury welled within Dick Wentworth. He knew what that thin wire signified, knew as well as if he had seen them, who was there in the shack with him.

He tugged hard at the wire, and jerked it out of the hands of the invisible person who had attempted to strangle him in the dark. There was a hissing, and a slithering movement of bodies, then suddenly there was ominous silence. Wentworth slid to his left, under the low wing of the plane. He made no more noise as he moved than did his silent attackers.

These men, he knew, were practicing an ancient evil cult of the East—the cult of the vicious Goddess, Kali, the cult of the *Thuggees*. If the thin, strong loop of wire had settled about his throat, Wentworth knew that it would have tautened instantly, would have cut deeply into his flesh, have constricted his arteries, and left him bloated, black in the face, dead.

These men were the pariahs of the Eastern world. How they had gotten to America was something that Wentworth wasted no time thinking about. He had traveled much in the East, and had heard weird stories of the little dark men who attacked unwary travelers in the night. These *Thuggees* could actually see and smell in the dark. They would be upon him again in a moment, with more of their deadly wire. And his means of defense were limited. He dared not shoot, for that would bring down upon him the uniformed forces of the law, who were hardly less a peril to him than the silent murderers lurking here.

RICHARD WENTWORTH

Thoughts tumbled swiftly through Richard Wentworth's mind, even as he acted. How had these men known that he would arrive here? He had told only one person of the probability of his using this landing field tonight. And that person was the one woman he loved—the woman who had risked her life countless times for him. It was unthinkable that she had betrayed him.

He had dropped flat to the floor now—he rolled over twice, away from the plane, and close to the wall. He could hear stealthy footsteps, moving around beyond the plane, in the space where the light car which he always kept here was stored. One, two, three pairs of footsteps he detected. There were at least three of them, perhaps more. They were stalking him, apparently secure in the knowledge that he dared not use firearms.

He was groping toward the toolbox, seeking for a wrench, or some heavy implement with which he might defend himself. His hand encountered the top of the box, lifted it open. The hinges creaked a bit, and he pushed the cover boldly all the way up, reached in gropingly. His hand rasped against the jagged teeth of a ripsaw, and he scraped the tips of his fingers. Involuntarily he raised his head, and too late realized his mistake. Without warning a gentle *swish* sounded, and a loop descended over his head, settled around his throat.

There was a hoarse, low cry of triumph from somewhere in the darkness, and the loop tightened with a sudden, vicious jerk that cut mercilessly into his throat. The thin wire was like the keen edge of a knife. Wentworth gasped for air as his breath was abruptly cut off, and his lungs began to feel as if they were filled with lead.

The line was being held taut by the unseen assailant. The loop of that wire would not be held by a tight knot, as in a cord, but in a loose slipknot that would give the moment the murderer stopped pulling. Yet it was useless to try to grasp that wire in his bare hands. It would only cut them, and not relieve the pressure. These Eastern *Thuggees* knew their business well.

The man at the end of the wire would be holding its end looped on a stick of wood or metal, so that he could pull at will against the soft skin of his victim's throat. There was no known defense against the garrote of these ancient Kali-worshippers. Not even a knife would cut through that wire in time to save a man from suffocating under its murderous pressure.

Already spots were dancing before Dick Wentworth's eyes. A gentle tug at the wire brought excruciating agony to his throat and lungs, and forced him to move his body in obedience to the pressure. And as he moved, his hand came out of the tool box with that ripsaw gripped tightly!

Richard Wentworth had lived all his life in an atmosphere of peril and quick-thinking action. Not once, but many times, his life and the lives of many thousands of people had hung upon an instant's decision made in the blink of an eyelash. Now, it was neither conscious thought or reasoned plan that caused him to slash in the darkness at the thin strand of wire that ran tautly from the noose about his throat to the hands of the invisible assailant. It was the reflex of the man who had earned his training in deadly clashes with the underworld, the instinct that had made all the actions of the Spider so feared and dreaded by criminals.

WHILE BREATH was suspended within him, while he gasped unavailing for air which did not come to his tortured lungs, Wentworth hacked at the wire with the keen teeth of the saw. Each time he rasped the blade over the wire, the pain at his throat was excruciating. The sharp grating noise was the only sound now in the shack. He had no means of telling whether the wire was giving or not—he only knew that he couldn't last more than a moment or two. As his arm worked frantically back and forth with the saw, his eyes became peopled with strange, fantastically colored figures in the darkness. Was this the forerunner of death?

These Eastern *Thugs* who were murdering him believed that the soul left the human body at death and chose another incarnation. Would his soul meet the soul of Tang-akhmut out there in the infinite, to fight again? Tang-akhmut had been a wily and ruthless opponent. These men were no doubt servants of his, acting upon his orders, even though he himself was dead for two weeks. What ironic destiny, that Wentworth should die by the orders of a dead man! Well, it was all over. There was no more air. The darkness was sparkling now with weird, fantastic colors. This must be death. Colors, revolving like pinwheels, mad dervishes in the air; a feeling of floating in infinite space; he was conscious—but was it the consciousness of death or of life? Was this his body or his soul that was aware of lights and colors and dizzy space—

Suddenly Wentworth became aware that great gulps of air were rushing into his lungs through a tortured throat! Fierce pains shot through his chest and his breath came in great, gasping sobs. The wire was no longer there. He had cut it!

Wentworth realized that he lay prone on the floor now, where he must have fallen when the pressure was released. With stiff fingers he felt of his throat, touched the loose loop of wire, touched wet and sticky blood. He was wheezing, sobbing with each breath. And to his ears came the soft pattering of miming feet—running *toward* him.

Richard Wentworth drove his battered faculties to meet the situation. The murderers were coming in to finish their kill. A dark shape moved above him—another, and still another. Guttural voices spoke monosyllabically. A knife gleamed in the darkness, and one of the forms bent low over him; the knife lashed down toward his throat. Wentworth summoned up the last ounce of his reserve energy, and rolled over on his back just as the knife drove downward with a vicious *swish.* It dug into the floor, missing him, and Wentworth uttered a hoarse low shout, and raised the ripsaw, slashed at the dark figure above him. The teeth of the saw caught in human flesh, tore through it, and there was a scream of pain. Again and again Wentworth slashed, and the figure fell away, gurgling. Two more figures bored in, and white teeth gleamed, knives lunged at him.

Wentworth twisted to avoid a point, and slashed up once more, in a wide swath. The two figures leaped backward, and Wentworth seized the opportunity, catapulted to his feet. His chest burned, his throat bled, and his breath still came in gulps. But he forced his perfectly conditioned muscles to respond to the impulses from his brain.

On his feet he swung the saw like a short sword, slashing at the two little dark, shadowy figures who closed in on either side of him. He backed away from the gleaming knives, lunged with the saw, and caught one of his assailants full in the face. The man tumbled backward with a screech of agony, dropping his knife and putting both hands to his eyes. The last of the trio did not turn to run, but bored in with deadly persistency.

These men were little, wiry, and slippery as eels. Wentworth's saw rasped across the man's sleeve, and the *Thug* ducked in, lunged upward with the point of the gleaming knife in a drive that was meant to disembowel Wentworth.

WENTWORTH SLID back, and the blade caught in his leather flying jacket. He dropped the saw, seized the knife hand, and twisted, heaving the man over his shoulder. The little *Thug* went into the air, hurtling with all the force that Wentworth had put into the maneuver. His body fairly flew through the air, ended up with the thudding crash of skull against concrete wall. The man's body crumpled, bounced to the floor.

Wentworth staggered, wobbling on his feet, bracing himself against further attack. There was none. From the floor came a low moaning of agony accompanied by the thrashing of a body.

Richard Wentworth leaned for support against the wall, and took out his pocket flash, clicked it on. The man he had struck in the face squirmed on the floor at his feet. It was he who was moaning. The other two were dead. Wentworth's face was grim as he knelt beside the wounded man. His nose and cheek were cut wide open, and blood had stained his clothes a deep red. The end of the saw had done dreadful damage; the nose was cut across the bridge, and the right cheek was gashed down to the chin.

Wentworth looked at him without pity. He poured the light of the flash directly into the *Thug's* bleeding face, and took the man's hands away.

"Who sent you here?" he demanded harshly.

The *Thuggee* looked up at him out of his slashed face with burning, hate-filled, almond eyes—eyes that did not blink in the light. The mouth under that monstrously wounded nose twisted into a hateful, leering curve. "The Master sent us, O Spider! Tang-akhmut, the living Pharaoh, the Lord of life and death, sent us to wait for you here and finish you!"

"You lie," said Wentworth. "Tang-akhmut is dead. I heard his death scream. You are a fool. You obey a dead man!"

The wounded *Thuggee* spat into the light. "It is you who are the fool, O Spider. Tang-akhmut never dies. We, who die for him, will live on in *Nirvana,* served by the spirits of those we have killed for the Master. I, and my two brothers, have failed here tonight. It is fitting that we should die. But you too, Spider, will die. There are others who will do the Master's bidding. There are many. You will die—soon after me!"

And the man seized the knife which he had dropped, and which lay beside him on the floor. Wentworth tensed to fend off the last desperate attack of the wounded man, but the *Thuggee* did not attempt to stab him. Instead, the man reversed the knife, resting the handle on the floor, with the blade pointing upward. Then he heaved himself up, and dropped straight down on the point of the knife!

The sharp blade entered his stomach, and he thrashed about on the floor, a gruesome spectacle. He rolled over on his back, and stared up into Wentworth's light. His face was transmuted into a gargoyle of hate and passion.

"I die!" he gasped. "But others will follow. The Master lives— and the Spider is doomed!"

And so the man died.

Wentworth stood a long time looking down at the body of the dead Hindu, bathed in its own blood. His own head was still reeling, and it still hurt him to breathe. These three had come terribly close to ending the career of the Spider here on the floor of this shack in Queens.

Wentworth was not concerned with the narrowness of his own escape. He was thinking of the last wards of the dying fanatic. The man had said that Tang-akhmut still lived. Was it possible that the sinister Man from the East had not died two weeks ago? Had it been another man's dying screams that Wentworth had heard? Suddenly the Spider felt weary and cold. He had thought that his task here in New York would be comparatively simple. But if Tang-akhmut still lived, then the whole dreadful fight must begin over again.

Tang-akhmut, the Man from the East, the man who called himself the Living Pharaoh, was the embodiment of all the forces of evil in the world. Who but Tang-akhmut would have had the diabolical cleverness to guess or to divine that the Spider would land here on his return?

WENTWORTH UTTERED a low curse, and stepped over the dead *Thuggee*, made his way around the plane and the automobile to the telephone. He dialed a number, waited breathlessly until he got his connection and heard the familiar, full-throated voice of Nita Van Sloan.

He thrilled at the sound of her voice. Nita was a weak spot in the armor of the Spider. Tang-akhmut had learned, somehow, that she meant more to the Spider than life itself. In the past, the sinister Man from the East had sought to hit at the Spider through her. If Tang-akhmut were back, he would surely strike again at Nita Van Sloan.

For a moment Wentworth was silent as Nita's voice came impatiently over the phone: "Hello, hello! Who's call—"

Abruptly Nita's voice trickled down to a whisper. She *knew* who was calling. Between these two there existed a subtle sixth sense that made speech almost unnecessary. Wentworth was convinced that there existed a whole cosmic series of thought-waves of which mortals were as yet unaware; and that he and Nita met somewhere on this infinite plane of thought transference because they were mystically attuned to each other.

How else was it that Nita knew with absolute certainty at that moment that it was Richard Wentworth who was calling her? It had been thus at the occasion of their first meeting. They had stood looking at each other in silence, not saying a word for what seemed an eon of time. And then she had smiled, and Wentworth had smiled; and he had said softly: "I'd been wondering how long it would be before we met!"

Nita had smiled in that slow, lazy fashion of hers, and they had walked off arm in arm, strangely intimate for two who had met for the first time.

Now, Nita's husky voice came once more over the wire: "Dick! You're—in trouble!"

She spoke it not as a question, but as a statement of fact. And Wentworth laughed shortly, reassuringly. "You're a couple of minutes late, Nita. The trouble is over—for the time being. Darling, I'm switching to Esperanto—in case your wire is tapped. I've a question to ask you."

"Right, Dick."

Long ago, Wentworth had taught Nita Esperanto, the international language originated by the Russian physician Zamenhoff. The language is exceedingly simple, embodying as it does only sixteen rules and a vocabulary of only three thousand words. Esperanto somehow has been neglected as a medium of communication, and they were safe enough in using it.

Now, Wentworth went on, using the international language as fluently as he spoke English: "Nita—*do you know where I am now?*"

"Why—no, Dick. I know you're near—"

"I'm at the emergency landing field—you know where it is. Think back carefully, Nita, because it's important *Have you mentioned this field to anyone recently?*"

"No, Dick, I haven't. To tell you the truth, I'd almost forgotten its existence."

"Well, some one knows about it. Three very pleasant little boy friends were waiting here to give me a reception."

16

"Dick! I knew—"

"It's all right now, Nita," he said grimly. "They won't do any more receptioning. But there's only one man I can think of who is clever enough to have found out about this place."

SUDDENLY NITA Van Sloan's voice became tense, vibrant. "You mean—"

"That's who I mean, darling, and nobody else!"

"But, Dick—he's dead. He was burned to death—"

"So I thought, Nita,—" he told her drily. "But one of the boy friends here just assured me that the man we're thinking of is still alive. They were here at his orders. *Do you understand what that means?* It means that you are in danger every moment of the day and night. Have you noticed whether you are being followed—"

"Trust me, Dick," Nita broke in. "I've watched carefully for shadows. There's one clumsy police shadow on my trail—I guess they hope I'll lead them to you eventually. I can shake him any time I want to. Outside of him, there is no one. But what do you intend to do, Dick?"

"I'm coming into Manhattan, darling!"

"You can't, Dick! The police are guarding every approach to the city. Every bridge and ferry, and every automobile road. The city is virtually under martial law. And that law seems to be dictated by some one who holds the officials in his power. They do nothing to stop the callous murders, the cruel crimes that are taking place every day. And the police seem to hate your name—I mean, they seem to hate the Spider—out of all proportion to the things charged against him. I think someone is inciting them against you, forcing them to hunt you. No one can get in or out of the island without passing through a cordon of police."

"I know, Nita, but that's all the more reason why I must come into the city. I had a plan to stop all that disorder. Of course, if Tang-akhmut is alive, the plan may not work. But I've got to try it."

"And then another thing, Dick. Some crank wrote a letter to the police department, and sent copies to all the newspapers, threatening to rob the vaults of the main office of the Finney Finance company tonight. And he signed your—he signed the Spider's name to it! Even if it's a forgery, the police aren't taking any chances. They're watching for you closely—"

Wentworth interrupted, chuckling. "It's no forgery, Nita. I wrote that letter!"

"But Dick! You're not actually going to *rob*—"

"That's what I plan to do. Believe me, Nita, it's impera-tive—all the more so if our ancient enemy is still alive. I've got pretty good information that Eustace Finney, and his Finance Company, were linked with Tang-akhmut."

"But how do you intend to get into the city?"

"With your help, Nita. Have you got the portfolio of enve-lopes I sent you by express from Cincinnati?"

"Yes."

Wentworth's voice crackled now as he issued instructions. "Take out the envelope marked number three. It contains a complete plan of procedure, except for the time element. You will follow those instructions in the minutest detail. Zero hour for the purpose of those operations will be midnight. If contact

18

is delayed at midnight; you will wait for me fifteen minutes, no more and no less. After that, if I have not appeared, you will know that the operation has failed, and you will at once proceed home and wait to hear from me. Is that all clear?"

"Yes, Dick, it's clear."

Characteristically, Nita did not ask superfluous questions, nor did she attempt to dissuade him from the undertaking. She was happy to be able to share his peril with him, to be of vital assistance.

"Good-by, dear," Wentworth said.

"Good-by, Dick, and good luck!" She almost whispered the last.

Wentworth broke the connection, and moved about swiftly, efficiently. For the time being he left the three bodies of the *Thuggees* where they were upon the floor. He moved into a small compartment separated from the rest of the floor by a closed-in partition, and shut the door behind him. Here he pressed a switch and clicked on the electric light, revealing a small, compact room with a dressing table, a rack of clothes, and a make-up mirror. He divested himself of his flying togs, seated himself before the mirror, and his long, capable fingers tended to the bloody scar around his neck. He used cotton and iodine with the swift efficiency of a practiced nurse, and soon he had the bleeding stopped. There was still a slight tremor in his lungs when he took a deep breath, but he paid it no attention.

Now he busied himself with tubes of make-up cream, and with plastic material in jars and boxes. Under his manipulations, the strong virile countenance of Richard Wentworth, which

19

stared back at him in the mirror, swiftly disappeared, giving place to sallow cheeks, elongated teeth, drawn-back lips.

A little kohl applied to the eyelids, and a drop of a concentrated reddish tincture from a small bottle, gave his eyes the appearance of deep, burning life. A wig of coal-black, matted hair completed the make-up, and Wentworth stared with satisfaction into the terror-inspiring face that was reflected in the glass—the face that had hundreds of times struck fear into the hearts of the underworld, and which was associated with the deadly pair of blazing guns that had so often exacted the supreme penalty from murderers and criminals in the crime-nests of the world. A black, waterproof cape and a low-brimmed black hat completed his attire, and Richard Wentworth was no longer in that room; he had given place to—the Spider!

Now the hatted and caped figure left the small make-up room, and went out into the garage once more. He got into the small coupé parked there, started the motor, and drove out toward what was apparently a blank wall opposite the big sliding doors through which the plane had been trundled. The wall slid back, acting also under the impulse of photo-electric rays, and the car moved out into a graveled path. The door in the wall slid closed once more, and the Spider drove out into the road, headed toward the East River.

Behind him, in the shack, lay the bodies of his three assailants. Before him lay high adventure, deadly peril. The Spider was moving to make good the challenge he had flung down to the police. He was going to enter the city through the guards and the cordons established to snare him. Everything depended upon the coordination and timing of his plan, and upon the cooperation of Nita Van Sloan. The least slip would mean his life, and perhaps much more. But there was no trace of hesitation in the attitude of the Spider as he drove toward the river!

CHAPTER 2
PERIL IN THE FOG

A HALF hour later, under cover of the dense fog that lay over New York, a small motor boat, with engine muffled, put out from the shore of Brooklyn and cut across the East River toward the dim, mist-encrusted skyline of Manhattan. The single occupant of the boat sat in the stern, guiding the light craft unerringly through the darkness. This man's figure was entirely covered by a dark cape, and his face was hidden by the brim of a turned-down black hat.

Beside him, a small radio sputtered on the short-wave band, and a police call began to come through: *"All cruisers and police launches! By special order of Deputy Police Commissioner Grant, there will be no reliefs at midnight. All crews will remain on duty through the night, supplementing the midnight shift. All bridges and approaches to Manhattan are to be watched, and all persons stopped and examined. A special reward of one hundred thousand dollars has been offered by an anonymous source, for the capture, dead or alive, of the person known as the Spider, in the event that he should attempt to enter the city tonight. Specific instructions will now be issued. Switch in your distorters for confidential orders...."*

Abruptly, the voice of the police announcer became a jumble

of hissing; shrieking noises. The new distorters that had recently been installed in many of the radio cars and launches made it impossible for an outsider to pick up the calls. Impatiently, the black-caped man twisted the pointer across the dial to Station WLNX. He gazed out through the heavy fog while News Commentator John Doane cut into the night from the radio, with the pithy, pungent comment that had brought him immense popularity almost overnight:

"Well, my friends, the big news of the night is that the Spider is coming back—and some lucky individual is going to collect a hundred thousand dollars reward for capturing or killing him! It is claimed that it would be absolutely impossible for the Spider to enter Manhattan tonight. Virtually every police officer in the city is on guard on the rivers and the bridges, and at every conceivable approach. The searchlights that you see from your windows, spotting the sky over Manhattan, are combing the air in case the Spider should attempt to land from a plane or parachute. Personally, my friends—" and John Doane's voice took on an edge of cultured distaste—"I would hesitate before trying to earn that hundred thousand of blood money. Yes, blood money. I have followed the Spider's career with interest, and I am convinced that he is not a criminal. The police are apparently subservient to some immense force of evil that has its tentacles in the city, and which is forcing them to hunt the Spider like a mad dog. And in keeping with my sentiments, I now issue this public message, whether the police or the sinister forces of evil in the city like it or not: *Spider, if you are anywhere within hearing of my voice, and if you should, by some miracle, enter the city tonight,*

I want you to call upon me for any aid or assistance you may need. New York is in the hands of a mob of madmen. All decent citizens will join with me in preferring your unorthodox methods to the evil forces which seem to control the police! Good luck to you, Spider!"

THE POWERFUL volume of Doane's eloquent voice rolled out over the foggy waters with such clarity and force that the man in the boat turned it down. He chuckled softly as Doane's comments continued; but in a moment he tensed, and spun the dial off, so that the radio lapsed into silence. Fingers of light from police launches were piercing through the fog on the river. Sirens were issuing raucous warnings, while the little boat kept its nose pointed steadily toward Manhattan, in spite of the clamor on the river.

But the thing that had made the man in the cape abruptly turn off the radio was the high bulk of a police launch which suddenly loomed darkly alongside, appearing without warning out of the fog. The police searchlight sprang into life and stabbed through the thick mist, settling on the figure of the man at the tiller of the motor boat. A shout went up from the police craft, as the cape and hat of the solitary boatman became starkly illuminated in the merciless glare of the spotlight.

For a moment the man raised his head, revealing the twisted features and elongated teeth under the matted black hair, and a great shout came from the lookout of the police launch: "The Spider! It's the Spider! We got him boys!"

There was a swift order from the commander of the launch. A rifle whined, and a slug whistled through the air, close to the boatman's black hat.

23

"You're covered, Spider. Put up your hands!"

The man in the boat stared full into the searchlight. His unnaturally hunched figure, his parchment-like skin drawn taut over high cheek-bones, and the snarling, thin lips twisted back from sharp teeth, were familiar to every policeman aboard the launch. Often they had glimpsed him in the years that he had fought crime in his own unorthodox fashion. Often they had seen him, slipping away from a gun battle with criminals where they themselves had arrived just a few moments too late. In the breasts of many of them there rankled a sneaking doubt as to whether the Spider was really an enemy of society, to be hunted to the death. But many crimes had been charged to this strange man's name, and there was a price upon his head—a reward to tempt the cupidity of any one. So, there was not a policeman aboard who would not gladly have given five years of his life for the honor and the reward of capturing the Spider. Now there was exultation in their voices as they clamored for him to surrender.

"Put up your hands, Spider!"

And the Spider seemed truly defeated, beaten, as he stood there in the boat, the merciless glare of the searchlight almost blinding him. His shoulders sagged, and his hands began to move upward, as if in obedience to the command. But suddenly, the slackness went out of him. With the blinding unexpectedness which had always characterized the Spider's movements, there appeared miraculously in each of his hands a blunt-nosed automatic. By some magic of legerdemain which remained a mystery to those men on the boat in spite of the spotlight trained on him, the Spider was firing, the two guns speaking as one.

Above the hoarse screams of the river sirens came the roaring, crackling explosions of his guns. He was firing, not at the police, but at the blinding center of the glare from the searchlight. No matter what those men in the launch might think of him, the Spider had never shot at an officer of the law in the just performance of his duty. And now, with liberty, and perhaps life at stake, he did not bring himself to violate that rule. The stream of lead from his two automatics lanced upward at an angle, in a fiery stream, and shattered the searchlight. Glass crashed, there was a spurt of fiery flame, and the beam of light disintegrated, dissolving into the thick, impenetrable fog.

THE SPIDER ceased firing, and deep silence descended for an instant upon the river while the dying echoes of the shots rolled back to them from somewhere in the north.

And then pandemonium broke loose aboard the launch. Men shouted angry curses, stamping about in the night like animals deprived of their prey. Half a dozen rifles began to bark savagely, pumping shot after shot into the little blotch of darkness where the motor boat rocked beside the police craft, at the spot where the Spider had stood in the boat. Had he remained there, his body would have been riddled by slug after slug. But the Spider hadn't waited for the fusillade of rifle fire. He had dived head-long over the side of his little boat, and he cut the water grace-fully, with hardly a ripple. The shots went harmlessly through the air, doing no damage, though one or two smashed through the sides and keel of the motor boat.

A dozen hand flashlights were focused over the side of the launch, and shouts of vindictive triumph went up when the empty, foundering motor boat was glimpsed. "We got him! We got the Spider!"

The flashlights swept the surrounding water, but there was no trace of the Spider. He was floating on the far side of the motor boat, his body almost entirely submerged, and his black waterproof cape billowing out around him to blend with the darkness as an effective camouflage. With the gloved fingers of one hand he clung to the gunwale of his boat. He waited thus motionlessly, while the muggy river lapped softly about him, tugging at the dark hat which covered the white oval of his face.

He held his breath, hoping that the launch did not have an auxiliary searchlight. The feeble rays of the hand torches would not betray him, but the bright glare of another spotlight would certainly dispel the fog around the boats sufficiently to show the police the floating figure of the man they were hunting. He could, of course, put out the second searchlight, if there was one, with a well-placed shot from the side of his boat. But he could never hope to escape the barrage of rifle fire that would surely engulf him once he gave his position away.

He heard the feet of the men tramping on the deck of the launch, and his body tensed in the water as he heard the commander order: "Switch in the auxiliary light! We've got to find his body!"

The Spider raised himself in the water a bit, by means of his grip on the gunwale, and drew one of his automatics. He could have shot out the light. But in the next instant his body would be riddled, and the Spider would be through. This was a poor way to die after all the perils he had fought his way out of in the past—like a cornered rat. They would haul in the bleeding body of the dead Spider, lay it, dripping wet on the deck, and celebrate. And the city would be given over to the vile plans of the Man from the East.

His gun was poised, ready for a shot at the searchlight the moment it glared into life. And then, a voice on board the launch called out to the commander: "I'm sorry, sir, there's no juice. When he shot out the light it caused a short. The transformer is scorched!"

The Spider breathed a deep sigh of relief, and sheathed his gun. It was at times like these that he often felt he bore a charmed life—a life immune to extinction until the cause to which he had devoted himself should be consummated. That cause was the total defeat of Tang-akhmut and the forces of evil which the sinister Man from the East had set alive in the city. The Spider had thought until tonight that Tang-akhmut was dead. He had thought that there remained for him only the task of wiping out the organization which the self-styled descendant of the Pharaohs had left in the city. But the attack on himself in the shack tonight, the report which Nita had given turn of conditions in the city, and the determined, vindictive efforts of

Wentworth was firing not at the police,
but at the blinding glare of the spotlight.

the police to capture him, together with the mysteriously anonymous reward offered for his capture, convinced the Spider that Tang-akhmut was not dead.

NOW HIS eyes glittered in the darkness when he learned that the auxiliary searchlight was disabled. The police launch was useless as far as searching for his body was concerned; they should logically return to shore to repair the light, and send another launch to seek his body. In that time, he could get back into the motor boat and move on to the meeting with Nita.

But a cold chill of doubt ran through his drenched body as he heard the next command from the launch: "You, Smallwood! Get down in that motor boat with a line and tie her to our stem. We'll tow it in as evidence that we killed the Spider! Then we'll fix the short and come back to search for his body!"

Men moved about on the launch, and the Spider floated motionlessly on his back, while the police craft was maneuvered alongside the motor boat. A uniformed policeman from the launch clambered down, and fastened a line to the smaller boat, then called out: "All ready, sir!"

The man, Smallwood, did not return to the launch, but moved toward the stern of the boat, and took the tiller. Had he looked over the side very carefully, he would have been sure to notice the black splotch which the Spider made on the surface of the water. But he did not. In a moment the engine of the launch kicked into life and headed toward the Manhattan shore. The rope tautened, and the motor boat stewed around in the wake of the launch.

The Spider's grip on the gunwale was almost torn loose by the sudden jerk of the boat, but he managed to hang on, keeping on his back. He was dragged along toward the shore. The siren of the launch was turned on full blast, and its raucous notes eddied in the air, drowning out all minor sounds. They were doing that out of sheer exuberance at having killed the Spider. They did not guess it at the time, but it was that very siren which was to enable the Spider to give them the slip!

Smallwood, the policeman in the motor boat, was a young man, only recently graduated from the Police Academy. He was flushed, excited at this adventure, and he stood up in the boat, balancing himself precariously. So absorbed was he with the excitement of the moment that he did not notice the dark figure that raised itself up by main strength from the water and slashed with a knife at the line that towed the boat.

Three times that hand rose from the water and slashed at the line before the policeman caught the flash of the knife. Then his eyes opened in amazement, and he shouted: "Hey! Stop—"

His voice was drowned by the shrill screaming of the launch's siren. He drew his revolver and scrambled forward, aimed down at the man in black. "Drop that knife!" he shouted ineffectually in vain competition with the siren. But the knife slashed once more, and the strands of the rope flew apart. The heavy pull of the launch did the rest, and the line parted just as Smallwood fired. The bullet kicked up the water far ahead of the Spider, and the sound of the explosion as well as of his voice was entirely lost in the siren's mad wail. Other sirens from the shore and from other patrol launches had added their din to that of the first.

The rope parted with a vicious *snap*, and the towing launch darted ahead.

Now was the moment that the Spider dreaded. The man at the tiller would feel the sudden acceleration of the launch, once it was freed of its tow. Would he notice it consciously—enough to cause him to investigate? Or would he be so keyed up by the excitement of the moment, so overwrought by the din and the noise that surrounded them, that its significance would not register with him?

If that launch turned back now, the Spider was lost. He could never hope to escape the concentrated fire that would be poured upon him from the police boat.

THE NEXT couple of seconds took on the forbidding aspect of aeons of time. The launch kept on its course while the Spider's heart beat rapidly, while Smallwood fired down at him five times in quick succession.

The shots missed, because the dark figure in the water was hanging on with both hands, and listing it far to port. The Spider's eyes were glued to the launch, with a fine disregard of Smallwood's shots. He was watching with held breath.

And the launch did not turn!

Its black hulk faded into the night, and the Spider was left alone on the river with the uniformed man in the boat. Now he pulled himself as far out of the water as he could, and the boat listed over at a dangerous angle. Smallwood, who had been trying to come forward to club the Spider, struggled frantically to retain his balance on the sloping keel. He uttered a despairing cry, and tumbled overboard! There was a loud splash, and the boat wallowed in the current. Smallwood's arms and legs beat frenziedly against the water, while the Spider climbed dexterously into the boat and seized the tiller.

The sirens were still shrieking, and no one in the launch had yet noticed that the boat was no longer being towed. The Spider peered over the side, saw Small-wood reaching wildly for the boat. The man's eyes gleamed with fright in the darkness, and his lips were agonizedly calling for help. The man couldn't swim!

The Spider's jaw tightened. His wrist watch showed twelve-five. Nita was to wait at the appointed spot only until twelve-fifteen. His need for speed now was urgent. If he delayed he might miss Nita. Also, the launch might at any minute discover that the tow-line was severed, and reverse its course. But the Spider had never yet made war on the police. He could not leave this man to drown, even if it meant capture. Grimly he kicked the motor into life, slipped the boat nearer to the struggling cop. Then he shut off the motor, reached over and gripped Small-wood's frantically reaching hand.

Before Smallwood fully realized what had happened, he had been thrust down into the bottom of the boat, manacled helplessly. He glared up at his captor, breathing hard. His lips twisted into a snarl, forming words which were lost in the din of sirens and fog-horns on the river.

The Spider paid him no further attention, but sprang to the tiller, slewed the boat around into the current.

Back under the bridge, the Spider cut off the motor and drifted with the current, his eyes straining forward through the fog. At last he sighted what he was seeking—a small blob of phosphorescence, hardly larger than a firefly, that seemed to be dangling almost motionless in space. Smallwood's eyes opened in wonder as he watched the Spider reach out toward the blob of light and grip a cable from the end of which it dangled. It was one of those little gadgets that are sold in five-and-ten cent stores to be attached on the end of light cords to enable them to be located in the dark. This one was hanging from the end of a long thin cable which was suspended from the upper structure of the Williamsburg Bridge!

The Spider kept his grip on the cable, and moved back to where the rookie cop sat. He had to raise his voice to be heard above the noise.

"I am leaving you here. The current will carry you back to the spot where the police boats are searching. If you sit quite still, you will be absolutely safe. Good-by, my friend!"

And leaving the cop to stare after him with wonderment and incredulity, the Spider seized the cable in both gloved hands, wrapped his legs around it, and hung there, dangling in the air. Smallwood shouted: "You're mad! You can't climb that—"

He halted, his eyes popping, his lower jaw hanging slack. Slowly, the cable began to rise, drawing its human, dark-cloaked cargo upward with it!

CHAPTER 3
KHANDRA VEG

W HEN NITA VAN SLOAN had finished talking
to Wentworth on the telephone, she went at once to
the wall safe in her apartment, and removed the packet she had
received only the day before.

Within the package were five envelopes, consecutively
numbered, and a short note.

> DEAREST NITA:
>
> I shall leave Cincinnati for New York within a day or two. I
> am writing a letter to the Acting Police Commissioner, in which
> I threaten to rob the vault of the Finney Finance Company.
> The reason for this strange threat I will explain in person when
> I see you. Of course, the police will place a careful guard over
> all the approaches to the city. In the enclosed envelopes there
> are outlined five different methods by which you can aid me to
> break through that guard. Keep them until I communicate with
> you, and I will then tell you which plan to employ.
>
> With love,
>
> DICK.

Nita hastily opened envelope number three, as Wentworth
had told her to do over the telephone. Her eyes glowed with
admiration as she read the concise instructions. She was to go to
the private laboratory which Wentworth maintained, and where
she had often worked with him. There she would find a number
of lengths of cable, which Wentworth had been engaged in test-

ing for tensile strength with a view to developing a new type of airplane strut. She was to load one of these coils in her car, and proceed to the Williamsburg Bridge. There she was to affix one end of the cable to the car, and drop the other end over the side of the bridge. She must be sure to select a cable which would reach to within a foot or two of the river, and she must attach a luminous substance to the hanging end. When she felt the tug of his weight on the cable, she was to drive the car slowly along the bridge, thus drawing in the cable after her.

Nita's slim, straight figure seemed to be charged with vivacious animation as she dressed hurriedly. Her quick mind comprehended Wentworth's plan at once. He would no doubt put out from the Brooklyn shore in one of the motor boats he had cached at various spots, and would find the cable under the bridge. Once on the bridge, the business of entering the city would be no problem at all, for the police guard was stationed at the Brooklyn end of the bridge, where all cars were stopped and the occupants questioned and examined. But all who passed the Brooklyn approach were not hindered in entering Manhattan.

She could not understand, of course, why Wentworth should want to rob the vault of the Finney Finance Company, and much less why he should have advertised it in advance. But she was sure that the Spider had a good and sufficient reason for doing things in just this way. As she put on a dark skirt and jacket of expensive, inconspicuous tailor-made material, her eyes became clouded for a moment at the thought of one of the things Wentworth had communicated to her on the phone—that Tang-akhmut was still alive.

If that news were true, it meant that all the work Wentworth and she had done, all the dreadful dangers they had came through in the last few weeks, were futile. Two weeks ago, in Cincinnati, they had breathed easier in the thought that the Spider's most ruthless and formidable adversary was finally disposed of. Tang-akhmut had woven an insidious web of terror in the consummation of his criminal objectives. The death and agony of hundreds of men and women meant nothing to the Man from the East. And he had used his weird organization of thugs and murderers in a merciless campaign to eliminate the Spider. Now, if he was back, he would be doubly dangerous, for Tang-akhmut's pride must have been mortally affronted by the defeat which the Spider had administered to him in Cincinnati. NITA FINISHED dressing, and took a small pistol from the night table, slipped it into her purse. Just then the bell of her apartment door rang. She frowned. It was ten-thirty, and she only had an hour and a half to keep her appointment with Wentworth. She stuffed his letter of instructions into her purse with the pistol, and hurried to the door, but did not open it. The bell was ringing again, insistently, and she slipped open the little peephole, looked through it.

The man who stood there was of medium height, but incredibly thin. His face was white, pasty, with the unhealthy pallor of the east. But in his black eyes there burned a fiercely evil light. He bowed when he saw that Nita was looking through the peephole. "Mith Van Thloan," he said with a pronounced lisp, "permit me to introduce myself. I am Khandra Veg, a humble servant of the living Pharaoh, Tang-akhmut. He sends me with a message for you. Please to open the door."

Khandra Veg stood there with his hands at his sides, an ironical smile curling his lips. The man might have been forty, or sixty—Nita had no way of telling. His body seemed shriveled, and there were folds of skin under his eyes. But there was poised deadliness about him, like that of the cobra. Nita was breathing quickly, a hand at her breast "Tang-akhmut," she said, "is dead. Has he sent you with a message from beyond the grave?"

She did not really think, any longer, that the Man from the East was dead. But she was sparring for time, wondering what had brought this emissary here at this moment. Her hand stole down to the purse she was holding, and she took out the small pistol.

Khandra Veg showed discolored, crooked teeth in a derisive smile. "You must know, dear lady, that Tang-akhmut still lives. Who else can have learned about the Spider's secret landing field in Queens? Come, Tang-akhmut is very much alive. And the message I bring from him is of great importance to you."

"Speak now," Nita commanded, "through the door."

He shook his head. "Tang-akhmut is the descendant of kings and emperors. His emissary must be received properly. Open the door. I am unarmed. If you have a gun you may hold it ready."

Nita stood still for a moment without speaking. She could not see to the right or left through the peephole, but she was almost sure that she had detected a faint hint of motion, a faint rustle from somewhere to the right of Khandra Veg. Her eyes flickered.

"Wait," she said. "I will put on some clothes and get a gun."

Khandra Veg bowed, his eyes twinkling triumphantly. "I wait!"

Nita closed the peephole. Then she raced swiftly through the apartment to the service door. While Khandra Veg waited at the front, she would escape through the rear. She had no time now to wonder what the emissary of Tang-akhmut wanted. She held the pistol ready, opened the service door on the safety chain, and peered out. She breathed a sigh of relief when she noted that the service corridor was empty. Directly across from her door was the door of the self-service delivery elevator. She darted across, pressed the button which would summon it up, and then turned swiftly, facing the stairs. If Khandra Veg or his men appeared either from above or below, she could cover them before they could see her. And she was a good enough shot to be able to keep them off till the elevator came.

She heard the rumbling of the elevator, heard it come to a stop in the shaft. With the caution that she had learned from Wentworth, she swung back the elevator door, thrusting her pistol ahead of her. But the elevator was empty. She smiled. Khandra Veg had overlooked a bet. It might even be that he had come with a bona-fide message. But she was not going to stay to find out. As soon as she was sure that the cage was unoccupied, she stepped in, shut the door, and moved over to the side where the buttons were located. She pressed the button for the basement, and as she did so, she felt some small object crunch under her foot. The cage was already dropping as she looked down at the floor to see what she had stepped on.

Too late she realized the trap she had walked into. There was a little brown pellet on the floor, and next to it the squashed remains of another, the one she had put her foot on. And the cage, was suddenly becoming heavy with a curious, terrifying odor. Her brain began to swim, her senses to clog. The strange Eastern incense that arose from the crushed pellet was numbing her mind, driving her into unconsciousness. She tore frantically at the collar of her jacket, seeking air.

The cage began to spin before her eyes, and then her sight was obstructed by a dark haze. The last thing she thought before she lost consciousness was that Khandra Veg had been sure she would not admit him; that he had deliberately appeared at the front door, so as to drive her to using the service elevator!

And then she crumpled to the floor in a pitiful heap, her bag, with the instructions from Wentworth, dropping at her side next to the pistol.

NITA'S NEXT conscious perception was of feeling a great lassitude, of overpowering peace. Her body seemed so light that it was in danger of floating up into the air if she did not anchor herself to something. She clutched at the sides of the object she was lying on, and opened her eyes. She was on a couch with a beautifully embroidered coverlet, in a room with soft light emanating from hidden sources. Rich hangings covered the walls, and a bowl of incense sent up a smooth plume of curling smoke from an inlaid stand beside the couch.

Nita knew that there was something terribly wrong here. She shouldn't be lying in the luxury and case of this room. Wentworth was going to miss her. She should be on the bridge, sending down a cable to pull him up. What was the meaning of this?

Suddenly her consciousness was shocked by the remembrance of the service elevator in her apartment house, of herself crumpling to the floor, smothered by that sick, sweet Oriental odor. She struggled up to a sitting position, and gasped, horrified to discover that she was nude, covered by nothing but a thin, soft-textured sheet. The sheet fell away from her body as she essayed to get to her feet, and she started back, pulled the sheet closely about her. For standing in the doorway, revealed as the rich hangings were pulled apart, was a man.

He was robed in a purple gown that hung to the floor, and from the turban on his head there gleamed a single huge jewel that fascinated her. The face of this man expressed tremendous power, tremendous evil. It was a long face, sharply etched. The high forehead spoke of strong mentality, and the deep, glistening eyes seemed to hold her with a queer force. Nita had seen that man before.

"Tang-akhmut!" she whispered, and drew the sheet tight about her, shrinking back on the couch from the malignance of his glance.

He smiled twistedly, and advanced into the room, walking with a smooth sinuousness on the deep, soft carpet.

"Welcome, Miss Van Sloan!" Tang-akhmut said in his deep, resonant voice. "I see that you remember me!" Behind him appeared a woman, lithe, supple, who much resembled The Man from the East. She wore wide pantaloons of transparent silk, and a silk jacket that was open at the front, revealing the soft curve of white breasts. She smiled wickedly behind Tang-akhmut, and spoke in a brittle, venomous tone:

"So this is the woman that the Spider loves! Let us see in what way she is more beautiful than I!"

And stepping close to the couch, the woman reached out and ripped the sheet from Nita's body. Nita was left uncovered. She did not shrink, but stared back at Tang-akhmut, and his sister, Issoris.

"She is beautiful, brother. But not as beautiful as I!"

Contemptuously Issoris threw back the sheet, and as Nita stood up, she wrapped it about her. She looked at Tang-akhmut. The Man from the East said smoothly: "I must apologize for depriving you of your clothes, Miss Van Sloan. My sister insisted on comparing your beauty with hers before you—er—die."

Nita stood calmly enough—outwardly.

"Your man, Khandra Veg, is very clever," she said. "He tricked me into getting into the service elevator. But you won't be able to trick the Spider so easily!"

The Man from the East laughed. "You are mistaken. The instructions we found in your purse are most enlightening. We have gone to the trouble of securing a length of cable and a car, just as the Spider ordered. He will find it hanging there for him at midnight, and will allow himself to be drawn up. Even then he will not suspect the trap, for my sister, Issoris, will be waiting for him beside the car. In the dark he will see only a feminine shape, and will think it is you. When he comes close to the car, it will be too late!"

Nita held herself tensely in check. In spite of her show of confidence, she realized that the Spider couldn't help falling into the trap.

TANG-AKHMUT CONTINUED speaking. "Of course, your wire was tapped, though my man couldn't understand the language you and the Spider used. But the written instructions gave me the whole story. I had you brought here for only one reason—I want you to tell me why the Spider chooses to rob the Finney Finance Company tonight, and why he announced it in advance. Can you tell me that?"

"I don't—know," Nita said very low. It was true that she didn't know, but Tang-akhmut would never believe it. His next words proved it.

He shrugged. "We have ways of persuading you to speak, Miss Van Sloan."

He clapped his hands, and two huge Nubians, naked save for loin cloths, appeared in the doorway. He spoke to them in a lilting foreign tongue, and they stepped forward, their black skin glistening darkly, and seized her by the elbows. Nita did not resist, for it would have been useless. Under the mocking gaze of the woman Issoris, she suffered herself to be led from the room.

Down a long corridor she was taken, then along another, into a small room. She uttered a gasp of anguish as she glimpsed the figure of the bearded man who was spread-eagled on the wall. The man's bronze skin was literally bathed in sweat, and he was biting his lower lip to keep from giving voice to the pain that wracked his body. The reason for his agony was the fact that a small vise made of strong metal was clamped across his body above the hips, in front of him. And a Nubian stood beside him, holding the handle of the vise. Each time the handle was tightened a notch, it constricted the body of the prisoner—until eventually it would crush every bone in his body.

Nita tottered in the doorway, and exclaimed through pallid lips: *"Ram Singh!"*

For this man was the Sikh servant of Wentworth, who had many times risked his life for his master and for Nita. Under the relentless hammer blows of Tang-akhmut's attack, Wentworth had been separated from his servants, had lost track of them. Here, then, was one of them!

Ram Singh forced a smile to his sweat-beaded lips, and his white teeth gleamed while his eyes rolled in agony. *"Wah, Memsahib* Nita!" he muttered. "The Snake from the East has caught you, too! It is bad!"

Nita would have run to him impulsively, but the two Nubians held her fast, grinning. She said: "Ram Singh! Why are they torturing you?"

The bearded Sikh laughed hollowly. "They wish you to do something for them, which will betray the master. And they think that the sight of me will soften you. But pay no attention, *Memsahib* Nita." He tried pitiably to straighten out his tortured body. "I am a strong man, and this is nothing!"

At that moment the smiling Khandra Veg entered the room, and Ram Singh's dark features were contorted with rage.

"Pig of an Egyptian!" he growled. "When I am released, I shall tear thy head from thy shoulders!"

Khandra Veg bowed mockingly to Nita, and motioned to the two Nubians who held her. They hustled her across the room to two pillars which rose to the ceiling. The pillars were about four feet apart, and they had rungs in them for hands and feet. In a moment Nita was spread-eagled between the pillars, just as Ram Singh was. One of the grinning Nubians approached with a vise like the one on the Sikh, and attached it to her white body.

Nita looked on, fascinated, as the Nubian, under Khandra Veg's direction, tightened the vise until the two clamps were pressing cruelly against her sides, making breathing difficult. Khandra Veg waved his hand, and the Nubians stepped back. His little eyes were gleaming with sardonic humor as he himself backed from the room.

"You are both ready now," he said. "My master, Tang-akhmut, the Living Pharaoh, will take care of your—er—entertainment from now on!"

THE DRAPE dropped behind him, leaving Nita in the room with Ram Singh and the Nubians. The vise about her body was so tight that she thought one of her ribs would break at any moment. She looked down and counted the threads which were visible on the spindle upon which the vise handle moved. There were fourteen of them. And there were still twenty or thirty more along which the handle could be turned.

By the time the handle had moved all the way along the spindle, the two clamps at her sides would almost meet—in her body. She glanced across at Ram Singh, and shuddered as she noted that almost three quarters of the spindle had already been traversed by the handle. No wonder there was sweat on his forehead!

Ram Singh was speaking to her in a low, self-accusing voice, punctuated by deep gasps as he sought to repress evidence of the agony he was enduring.

"*Memsahib* Nita, I am a low, base thing. I allowed myself to be tricked and captured by the little men of this Snake from the East—not without dipping my knife in the blood of many of them first. But their numbers were too great for me. And when I was brought here, the Snake tried to make me speak. He gave me a strange drug, and asked me questions, and I—I answered them!"

Nita demanded tensely: "What did they ask, Ram Singh?"

"They wished to know where my master would come if he traveled from the west. They asked if he had a landing field anywhere nearby. God forgive, I told them about the field in Queens. Even while I spoke I tried to stop, but the cursed drug was the stronger!"

Nita smiled wryly. "It is not your fault, Ram Singh. I, too, was tricked. And now, Tang-akhmut knows where I was to meet Dick, and Dick will surely fall into a trap—"

She broke off as the curtains were parted once more, and Tang-akhmut appeared in the doorway, with Issoris just behind him. The Egyptian princess was dressed in the dark tailored suit that Nita had worn, and in the dim night she might almost have been mistaken for Nita.

Tang-akhmut strode into the room, and the Nubians prostrated themselves. The Man from the East stood before Nita, and spoke quickly, imperiously.

"Miss Van Sloan, for the last time—will you tell me why the Spider goes to rob the Finney Finance Company?"

Nita regarded him scornfully. "I told you before," she said quietly, "I don't know."

Tang-akhmut stirred impatiently, and motioned with his hand. One of the Nubians moved across to Ram Singh, and turned the handle of the vise. The clamps moved together a fraction of an inch, and a spasm passed across the Sikh's face, to disappear instantly under his iron self-control. He gasped: "It is nothing, *Memsahib* Nita. Do—not—speak!"

Nita almost screamed: "Leave him alone, you devil! I tell you, I don't know! I don't know!"

Issoris, behind her brother, smiled queerly, a strange light of fascination in her tawny eyes as she viewed the Sikh's agony.

Tang-akhmut stepped close to Ram Singh, and spoke slowly: "Sikh! Tell your mistress to speak before your body is crushed like an eggshell. You will be cast forth, a miserable, broken man, to beg in the streets. Tell her to speak!"

Ram Singh raised his eyes to Tang-akhmut, and slowly straightened, though the effort must have cost him untold agony. Then, calmly, he spat into the face of the Living Pharaoh!

Tang-akhmut recoiled, and his face purpled with fury. He wiped his mouth with the sleeve of his robe, and shouted in a strangled voice to the Nubians:

"Tighten it! Tighten the vise! Break him!"

But that last movement of defiance had been too much for Ram Singh. His bearded head dropped upon his chest, and his body sagged in its bonds. He had fainted!

Tang-akhmut, still furious, shouted: "Bring water! Revive him! He must feel every moment of this agony!"

47

But Issoris gently pulled at his sleeve. "You forget, O Brother, that Wentworth comes to the bridge at midnight. It is already half an hour after eleven. We must be there to let the cable down for him, otherwise he will think that his beloved"—she smirked toward Nita—"has failed him. Come! We can attend to these two later."

Tang-akhmut slowly brought himself under control. "Good!" he granted. "You will bring Wentworth here, and let him witness the death of both of them! Go with Khandra Veg—and do not fail!"

As they passed through the doorway, Issoris turned, smirked tantalizingly at Nita.

"I go," she said, "to meet your lover!"

CHAPTER 4
TRICKY PRINCESS

"And if thou readest the other page, even though thou inert dead and in the world of ghosts, thou couldst come back to earth in the form thou once hadst!"

From the Book of Thoth.

SLOWLY THE cable rose, while the caped figure of the Spider clung to it, swaying in the air. The fog had become so thick that the Spider could no longer see the manacled figure of the policeman in the boat below. Fog horns and sirens were still screaming. Long probing searchlights were playing on the dark waters of the East River, seeking the body of the Spider; and here he was, rising steadily into the air.

As he neared the span of the tall bridge, Wentworth peered upward. His legs were twined around the cable, and his gloved hands gripped it above. It swayed from side to side with his weight as it rose, and Wentworth had the uncomfortable sensation of being suspended in midair in darkness far above the river.

His legs tightened, and his hands grasped the cable more firmly. There was very little cable to spare below his legs. If he should slip, he would go hurtling down into the darkness, to be smashed into the muggy water below.

The swaying of the cable increased, and sudden dizziness assailed him. His weight began to prove a tremendous strain against the muscles of his arms and legs. For he himself was a hundred and eighty pounds of bone and muscle; but in addition to that his clothes were soggy and dripping from his immersion in the river, and that added weight had to be supported.

From above he began to hear the sharp, rasping sound that the cable made against the bridge girder around which it had been slipped. He closed his eyes to drive back the brightness as the cable swayed more and more. It was moving up with entirely too much speed.

Nita, he thought, must be excited, or there might be danger threatening. Suddenly he stiffened as he clung to the cable. He was *sure* that there was danger somewhere.

He opened his eyes. He would have to watch for the top. At the speed with which the cable was rising, he would have

His jaw hardened at the sight of the trap he had barely avoided.

to move fast when he reached the top, or he would be literally brushed off when the cable swished around the girder.

Cautiously he loosened one hand, raised it, ready to seize the first hand-hold that offered on the bridge. His legs slipped a bit downward along the cable, and he felt the end of the line slipping up between his feet. He quickly brought his hand back to its grip, drew himself up another inch, and twined his legs around once more.

Now he was nearing the top, and the girders of the bridge seemed to be rushing down at him with express-train speed. Surely Nita must know that he would be smashed by those girders before he could grip them! Why didn't she slow up?

And then, suddenly, the cable stopped moving! There were still some three feet between his reaching hands and the lowest girders. He would have to raise himself that distance. Slowly the cable ceased swaying, and Wentworth began to worm upward, inch by inch, hoisting himself by his arms, then twining his legs, resting a moment, then hoisting once more. His eyes, under the black hat, were raised to the bridge, for a sight of Nita.

She should be coming back from the car now. He knew her well enough to know that she wouldn't wait there for him, but would come to see if she could lend a hand. And that foreboding of danger still chilled him. But he worked on, finally raised himself so that he could grip the girder around which the cable had been slipped.

He raised both hands to clutch the girder, and loosened his legs, allowing the cable to swing free. Now he hung suspended over the river far below—hung by his hands alone. He gripped hard, kicked back, then swung his legs forward until his feet caught a hold on the girder. In a moment he had heaved himself over on to the bridge. He was on solid footing at last!

He rested on one knee for a moment while he breathed deeply, and slapped his arms across his chest. They were almost numb, for the blood had not been able to circulate freely while he had them raised over his head. While he regained his breath and drove the blood back to normal circulation, he peered toward the Manhattan side, seeking the car. Some two hundred feet ahead he glimpsed the tail lights, saw a feminine figure in a dark suit standing behind the car. He frowned. Why didn't Nita come to meet him?

CARS WERE passing on both lanes of the bridge, but Wentworth was off on the edge, on the outside of the girders, and he was not noticed. Once his arms had lost their numbness, he worked swiftly taking off his hat and cape. Rolled up, they made a comparatively small bundle, which was hardly noticeable.

He removed the false teeth from over his own, the plates from his nostrils and the wadding from under his lips. In a matter of seconds, the Spider had disappeared; but the artificial face coloration remained, together with the wig. And though he was no longer the Spider, neither was he Richard Wentworth.

He peered ahead, saw the figure of the woman he thought was Nita, still waiting beside the car. He did not suspect at this time, that it was not Nita; but he *did* think that there was something wrong—perhaps that Nita had not been able to shake off some trailer, perhaps that she had been followed to the bridge, and was therefore keeping her distance from him. He knew very well that if everything had gone according to schedule, Nita Van Sloan would have run to him the moment he appeared over the side of the bridge.

So he did not make the mistake that a thousand men in similar position might have done—he did not go directly to the car. The time he had taken to remove the traces of the Spider from his appearance had been so short that it aroused no suspicions. Now, he coolly took out his guns and checked them to make sure the water had not fouled them. He holstered them once more, and dropped flat on his face.

Then he agilely swung himself over the side of the bridge, allowing himself to hang once more by his hands from the girder. And in that position he moved, inch by inch along the girder, working himself over toward the car. If Nita had been followed, or if anything else were wrong, he meant to know about it before he showed himself. It was this extra ounce of caution in all the activities of Richard Wentworth that had kept him alive to this day.

With his feet dangling in the air, the whole weight of his body on his hands, the trip along the girders was no easy task, even for a man in the pink of condition. But be finally managed to reach a spot alongside the car, and gripping the girder tightly, chinned himself up so that his eyes were above the level of the bridge. And his jaw hardened at sight of the trap he had barely avoided.

Close beside the running hoard of the car, two men crouched. They were thin, wiry, dark-skinned men of the East. And each held a leather-thronged blackjack. They were in the shadow,

Two policemen were already clinging
to the swaying trolley in which
the Spider was escaping.

so that if Wentworth had approached the car from the rear, as they expected, he would never have noticed them. Their whole attitude as they crouched in the darkness, tautly, spoke of their deadly intent.

Peering past them, Wentworth could see the smartly tailored feminine figure that stood expectantly near the tail-light, straining to catch a glimpse of him at the spot where be had come up over the side. At first, Wentworth thought that it was Nita, and that she was somehow under the influence of these dark men.

He also saw a thin-lipped man sitting at the wheel of the car. He did not know him at the time, having never seen him before. But in a moment he saw the woman turn around and move toward the front of the car, past the two crouching Egyptians. She leaned in at the window, and spoke to the man at the wheel.

"Khandra Veg," she said, "I think that the Spider is too smart for us. He has climbed to the bridge, but I cannot see him, for he is in deep shadow. And he comes not!"

Wentworth caught a glimpse of the woman's profile as she spoke, and he repressed a gasp. He recognized Issoris, the beautiful, feline sister of Tang-akhmut. Not so many weeks ago he had been face to face with this woman, and she had offered herself to him—and Wentworth had spurned her. Now, he doubted not that she hated him even more than did Tang-akhmut.

It was a shock to see her here. And sweat broke out on his forehead—sweat that he could not wipe off at the peril of dropping hundreds of feet into the river below; for the full implication of Issoris' presence here struck him like a hammer blow. It meant that Nita must have been captured by The Man from the East—must even now be a prisoner somewhere in the city, while Issoris came to capture the Spider, too!

WENTWORTH'S LIPS hardened, and he gripped the girder more tightly. The strain upon his arms was becoming terrific, but he dared not move, for Khandra Veg was speaking in his slow, oily voice.

"It is too bad, Princess of the Faith; the Spider must have good eyes, and he may have detected that you are not the other girl. I will send the two hunters to find him. Perhaps they will have to kill him—"

"No, no!" she hissed, fiercely. "I want that man alive! I want him to squirm while he watches the pale girl whom he loves—watches her gasp and shriek upon the torture rack. I want him to beg me on his knees to spare her. And then—" the malevolence in the voice of the Pharaoh's sister was ghoulish "—then I will crush the life from that girl, and laugh at him!"

Khandra Veg shrugged. "As you command, Princess!" He spoke sharply, in a dialect that Wentworth did not understand, to the two crouching men. They grunted, melted into the darkness in the direction of the spot where the cable lay. The woman, Issoris, got into the car beside Khandra Veg. "The Spider will think that I lose patience, and depart," she said. "Then our men will fall upon him."

The rest of what she said was lost upon Wentworth, for he had gotten into motion the moment she entered the car. Exerting every last ounce of his great reserve strength, he drew himself up over the girder upon which he hung, and crawled on his stomach to the right of the car, squirmed under it, and came up on the other side. Swiftly he put a hand on the rear door, twisted the handle and yanked the door open.

He sprang inside, shut the door behind him, and had his two guns out before Khandra Veg and the woman could turn around. He pressed the muzzle of a gun against the neck of each, and said grimly:

"The Spider greets the sister of the Pharaoh. You, Khandra Veg, will drive this car along the bridge. You will drive swiftly, or I will fire a bullet into the base of your neck!"

Khandra Veg sat quite still, his hands on the wheel. Issoris half turned, and her green eyes met those of Wentworth.

"Greetings, Spider," she said. "You are a very clever man!"

Wentworth disregarded her, but he kept the muzzle of his gun pressed hard against her neck.

"Drive, Khandra Veg!" he ordered.

Khandra Veg still did not move. Wentworth, looking into the rear vision mirror, saw a disdainful smile upon his lips. "Shoot, Spider," he said. "I do not fear to die. My master, the living Pharaoh, has read the pages of the Book of Thoth. He will bring me back to life! He has promised!"

Wentworth looked at the man unbelievingly. "You—are ready to die for your master?"

"Why not? Death is not permanent—to those who know the secrets of the gods. And my master, Tang-akhmut, the Living Pharaoh, whose sister, the Princess Issoris, sits here beside me, knows how to bring back the dead to life!"

Wentworth nodded speculatively. He could understand now why Tang-akhmut commanded such implicit obedience—even to the point of death—from his followers. He had revived an ancient legend; and these Egyptians had swallowed it, hook, line and sinker. The legend of Thoth,* the ibis-headed recorder of the gods, was as old as Egypt—nay, older. And it was not strange that these people should be ready to give it credence today.

It was the same fatalism that Wentworth had often met in the East—the same belief in a future existence on this earth which actuated so many Eastern peoples to deeds of almost unbeliev-

---

* AUTHOR'S NOTE: Even today, the ancient legend of Thoth receives credence in many far-flung corners of Egypt. It is related that Thoth wrote down the secrets of his gods in a book which was placed at the bottom of a river, and guarded in many boxes of different metal, one within the other, and that the boxes were surrounded by "snakes and scorpions and all manner of crawling things, and above all a snake which no man can kill." A certain king's son was tempted by a renegade priest to go in search of the Book of Thoth, for then he would know all the magic of the world. It was said that if one read the first page, he would be able to command the earth and the sky and the mountains and the sea, and that he would understand the language of all the creeping things of earth. But if he read the second page, even though he were dead and in the world of ghosts, he could come back to earth in the form he once had—and that he would even behold the shapes of the gods! According to the ancient legend, the king's son succeeded in wresting the Book of Thoth from the bottom of the river where it lay heavily guarded, and though the gods took vengeance, the Book forever after remained the property of the kings of Egypt—thus giving them the power of gods. It was entirely possible, therefore, for men to believe that one who claimed to be the Living Pharaoh, should know the secrets of Life and Death.

able sacrifice. He could see that Khandra Veg would never obey him under the threat of death.

But every minute was vital. Those two Egyptians would return to the car, to report that they could find no trace of the Spider. He would have to fight them with blazing guns, and the police would come. The Spider would be captured entering the city, and Tang-akhmut would hold Nita at his mercy.

WENTWORTH KNEW that Issoris guessed what was passing through his mind, and this was confirmed when she said mockingly: "You are a fool to pit yourself against the Lord of Life and Death, Spider! Throw down your guns and place yourself at my brother's mercy!"

Wentworth regarded him coldly. "I hate to do this," he said, "but this is war, and everything goes." Suddenly his voice hardened, and the blue barrel of his gun bored into the white skin of the Princess' neck. "You will order Khandra Veg to obey me, or I'll let *you* have the slug. Let's see if you have enough faith in that brother of yours to take a chance on his bringing you back to life! Now quick—you have one minute!"

Issoris' dark eyes narrowed, and her red lips curved in a forced smile. "You would shoot—a woman?"

Wentworth's eyes did not soften. "You have three-quarters of a minute!"

The Princess shuddered slightly. "I—believe you'll do it!"

Wentworth didn't answer. His eyes never left hers. His face, grim and unrelenting, did not reveal the turmoil that was going on within him. After all, Issoris was a woman—and a beautiful woman. That there was a devil of evil within her breast, that her soft, beautiful body was but a mask for the mad passion for power that ruled herself and her brother, did not matter. Wentworth could only see that when he pulled the trigger, it would blast out the life from that soft body. Could he do it? Once before he had had her at his mercy—and he had let her go. Could he do it now? *Could he do it now?*

If she laughed at him, he was lost. Khandra Veg would not move. The two Egyptians would come up to the assistance of the Princess....

Wentworth would never know whether he could have brought himself to pull the trigger that would have sent a leaden slug into the spine of the Princess Issoris. For she saved him the trouble of a decision. Slowly, her eyes dropped before his.

"I know—" she gasped—"you would do it!" She closed her eyes, spoke in a low voice to Khandra Veg:

"Obey him, Khandra Veg!"

Wentworth sighed in relief as the Egyptian shifted gears obediently, sent the car rolling toward Manhattan. He was not out of the woods yet, by a long shot. He could see the sharp, calculating features of Issoris, lit up by some secret triumph; she was laughing at him.

Why? *Why?* There was something he had overlooked—there must be something his calculations had missed. Khandra Veg drove slowly, smugly. He, too, knew the secret that made Issoris laugh. Wentworth was taut, thinking rapidly. The speedometer read eighteen, nineteen....

Wentworth bored hard with the barrel of his right hand gun at the smooth skin of the Princess. "Tell your man to speed it up.

Step on the gas. Bring it up to forty!" He had remembered that those two Egyptians who had gone out in search of him were wiry, hard men. They could no doubt run fast—fast enough to catch the car at the slow rate that it was being driven.

"Speed it up!" he ordered.

Issoris said softly, mockingly: "Obey the gentleman, Khandra Veg. Give him more speed!"

The Egyptian nodded, stepped on the gas, and the car accelerated swiftly. And suddenly, from behind them, there came a whistling, screaming sound. The cable! Wentworth knew now why Issoris was laughing. The cable still trailed them. The car was swinging from the ramp of the bridge now, into crowded Delancey Street. That cable, singing and whistling behind them like the whipping tail of a comet, would call the attention of every policeman on the street. They'd be stopped!

"You see, Mr. Spider," the Princess taunted, "it will do you no good to shoot me. See, already a police officer is raising his hand for us to halt. See him tugging at his gun? Well, Mr. Spider, will you shoot the policeman? Or will you allow him to arrest you? You know what awaits you at police headquarters—a cell, and a trial for murder!

"Make up your mind quickly. Give me your word to surrender to my brother, and I will explain to the satisfaction of the officer. You can sit in the back of the car, and I will talk. The officer will accept any explanation, for I have a card from the deputy commissioner. My brother has great—influence in the city. Speak quickly. The tables are turned—you have less than a minute!"

CITY OF DREADFUL NIGHT

THE CAR had slowed up in the crowded street, and the cable was flapping behind, tangling with other cars. It would be only a matter of seconds before it became hopelessly meshed with other cars, and they would be brought to a halt. And there, less than twenty feet ahead at the corner, a traffic officer had pulled out a service revolver and was blocking their path. At the same time another bluecoat was running toward them from the curb, blowing a whistle, also tugging for his revolver. So tense had the city become under the wave of crime that had swept over it that policemen no longer waited for actual threats to their lives, as the regulations provided, before drawing fire arms. Of late, they had been wont to shoot at the slightest provocation, and to ask for explanations later.

Wentworth knew that he was in a cleft stick. He must either take his chances with the police, or surrender to Tang-akhmut's sister. If he gave his word now, he must go through with it. It never entered his head that he could promise, and then break that promise. Throughout the underworld it had become an axiom that the Spider's word was better than a bond. And if he promised now to surrender, he would do it. Issoris knew that, and she would take his word.

The wheels of the ear scraped, dragged against the cable, which had become snagged in the cars behind them. Their auto ground to a stop, facing a trolley car moving north on the Bowery. The traffic officer and the bluecoat from the curb bore down upon them. Khandra Veg sat still, clutching the wheel. Issoris looked up at Wentworth, and her lips parted provocatively. He could see her breast heaving with the anticipation of victory. "Well, Spider? Choose—between the police and Tang-akhmut!"

Wentworth's eyes bored into hers. "I choose—neither!" he grated.

With a swift movement, he wrenched open the door of the auto, and leaped out on the far side from the approaching policemen. Issoris screamed after him:

"You fool! You've chosen death!" Then she raised her voice and shrieked, "It's the Spider! The Spider! Get him!"

The crowd that had gathered at the curb took up the shout. The revolvers of the bluecoats began to thunder, and slugs ricocheted from the pavement before Wentworth. He had landed on his hands and knees, still gripping both guns. He crouched low, raced straight across the street toward the open trolley car, which was stopped on the crossing, under the "L" structure on the Bowery.

More bullets were whining after him now, for Khandra Veg was also firing from the car. But Wentworth weaved and crouched, reached the trolley and leaped up beside the motorman. Police whistles were shrilling madly, and bullets were still following Wentworth. It was a testimonial to the wretched state into which the city had degenerated that the police officers did not stop shooting even when their shots endangered the life of the driver of the trolley car and of the four passengers in the cross seats behind him. The motorman ducked as a shot whizzed past Wentworth's shoulder and smashed into the glass window.

He turned a startled face to Wentworth, dropped to his knees, and hopped off the far side of the trolley. The passengers gave way to wild panic, and followed the example of the motorman. In a trice, the trolley was emptied, leaving the Spider in sole possession. That possession was no sinecure, for the street was resounding to the reverberations of half a dozen revolvers now, those of the two bluecoats and of Khandra Veg having been reinforced by the guns of the crew of a radio car that had swung into Delancey from the river front.

Wentworth swung about with tight lips, faced the car from which Khandra Veg was shooting, and snapped a shot at the windshield. His slug failed to crack the bullet proof glass, and Khandra Veg hastily drew in his head as Wentworth sent another shot at him. The bluecoats were closing in on the trolley now. In a moment they would be within pointblank range, and could not miss him.

WENTWORTH COOLLY holstered both guns, and seized the controls of the street car. The motorman had left the power on, but when he had leaped from the car he had taken his foot from the safety brake, which automatically broke the circuit and stopped the car. Now Wentworth depressed the safety brake with his foot, and swung the power handle around to wide open position. The trolley creaked, dragged, and spurted ahead on the tracks.

The two bluecoats were racing alongside the trolley now, and firing as they ran. The bullets sang around Wentworth's head as he crouched at controls.

The traffic officer shouted to the other bluecoat: "Jump in, Reilly!" and leaped aboard himself.

Reilly, whose gun was empty now, leaped on behind the traffic officer and both policemen clung to the wildly swaying trolley. Ahead, the tracks lay empty for a mile, as traffic hurried to get out of the way of the racing street car. Behind, the police radio car swung into the chase, and behind it, a line of other cars with volunteers in this hunt for human game; for the Spider was considered fair game, and the average man always thrills to a manhunt.

Wentworth looked in back, saw the two bluecoats climbing aboard. He saw the traffic officer level his revolver at him. The man did not call to him to surrender. He was taking no chances. The reward for the Spider read: *"Dead or Alive!"* and he was going to bring in a dead Spider. Wentworth dropped to one knee, just as the bluecoat pressed the trigger. But no shot crashed out. The traffic officer cursed. His gun was empty. He had emptied it in the street, without counting his shots. Reilly, the other cop, shouted: "Mine's empty, too, Baker. Come on, let's take him!"

BAKER, THE traffic officer, was already at the front of the car, about to step up on the platform. Reilly was close behind him. Wentworth kept his foot on the pedal, and the car sped crazily along the screaming tracks.

Wentworth raised one of his guns, pointed it at Baker's head. "Stand where you are!" he shouted.

Baker was no coward. "Go to hell Spider!" he yelled, and moved forward, reaching to grip the handlebar of the platform. Wentworth's eyes showed admiration for the man's courage. He did not fire. Instead, he stooped swiftly, and took his foot off the brake pedal; then gripped it with his hand and ripped it off the spring.

With the sudden cutting of the power circuit, the brakes squealed, and the trolley lurched to a groaning halt. The sudden stop almost flung Baker and Reilly from their foothold on the running board, and gave Wentworth the extra moment of respite that he needed.

The wheels screeched in protest, but held against the tracks. The trolley slowed down. The square here was a mess of dotted traffic, cars and trucks having herded off toward the curb to get as far as possible from the hurtling juggernaut. The street was crowded, jammed with pedestrians, who watched with mouths agape. Wentworth did not wait for the car to come to a halt. He leaped to the ground and darted between two trucks, while the pursuing cars screamed up behind, and Baker and Reilly leaped to the ground.

Cries went up: "The Spider! The Spider is escaping! Kill the Spider! Kill! Kill!"

Frenzied men, hot with the sudden fever of the manhunt, closed in on the spot where Wentworth was twisting in and out of cars and trucks. A crazed, blood-lusting, fanatical mob leaped in to the kill. And Wentworth wriggled out from behind a truck, sped across the street toward the narrow alleys of Chinatown which opened out from Chatham Square. At his heels the insensate mob bayed its paean of hatred and bloodlust.

Shots cracked behind him, slugs whined madly, fired without aim. A man cut across in front of him, to stop his flight, and Wentworth straight-armed that one, sent him reeling, and sped into the dark narrow blackness of Doyers Street, with the pack streaming after him. Now, Wentworth knew what it truly meant to be a hunted thing, with the hand of every man against him. Here were ordinary citizens, men who never dreamed of battle and sudden death, blood-hungry on the track of a man they had never met.

Many of those who chased him tonight might have been dead today if the Spider had not fought mightily in their behalf, if he had not placed his own life, and the lives of those he loved in jeopardy for their sakes. But they didn't know about those things, and even if they had, all that would not have counted tonight, when they were aroused by the primordial lust for the hunt.

Wentworth twisted in and out of alleys, never more than a yard ahead of his pursuers. The night favored him, and his dark clothes, and the close compactness of his pursuers. Also, there was the selfish desire to be the first to capture the Spider. Men in that pursuing throng jostled each other out of the way, tripped each other, in order to get in the lead.

And Wentworth fled. He wanted very dearly at that moment, to stop and turn to face the baying pack, with his two guns blazing in his hands. Every fighting instinct within him urged him not to flee, but to stand and fight. He could mow down that close-packed throng behind him, stop them, even make them turn and flee. The Spider had done that before, with hardened criminals. How much easier he could do it now, with these crazed citizens who did not even suspect that he was armed. And so, as he used every ounce of his strength to duck and twist and flee, Richard Wentworth fought out a battle with himself that he had fought hundreds of times before. Why should he forbear to fight these men who sought his blood? They were blind, foolish creatures, who would destroy the one man who did not stint himself in their behalf. If he killed a dozen of them, what would it matter?

WENTWORTH CLENCHED his teeth, and forced himself to flee. These men who hunted him might be blind and foolish—but they were not criminals. They were *innocent*. And Wentworth had never shot down an innocent man. For that forbearance, Wentworth might pay with his life tonight—the very next moment, in fact. But he would never cheapen his principles. If he died, he could face his God with his head held high....

Strange, what jumbled phantasmagoria of thought can race through a man's mind in the split-instant of deadly peril. A rock hurtled past his head, thrown by some one in the crowd at his heels. A hand reached for his coat, gripped it and lost it, so close were they. Wentworth twisted to the right into an alley between a Chinese curiosity shop and a lychee nut store.

The momentum of his yelling pursuers carried them past the alley before they could stop, and Wentworth raced down the ally a few steps, stopped and reached for a row of ash barrels that stood along the wall. He whirled them out, tipped them over, in the middle of the alley, then turned and raced down toward the blackness at the farther end.

The mad crowd pressed in after him now, police shouting loudly for the others to get out of the way so they could fire down the alley. But the men in the crowd pushed on, stumbled over the ash barrels, and piled upon each other. Wentworth reached the end of the alley. A blank wall rose up in front of him. To the right was a doorway, almost indistinguishable in the night. He had not come here at random. He knew where that doorway led. And he knew that there would be someone there to answer the peculiar knock that he repeated twice upon the rotting wood of the door.

Strangely, in the mad race through Chinatown, few of the yellow residents had shown themselves. Those who had been in the street had not joined in the chase, had not attempted to stop the fleeing man. In fact, they had seemed utterly disinterested. Nevertheless, swift news had flown through the section of what was occurring.

Somehow, by the strange grapevine of the Orientals, it was known that the Spider was being hard-pressed, was fleeing for his life. And now, when Wentworth rapped, a door opened instantly. Almost it seemed that his coming had been expected, awaited.

CHAPTER 5
WANG CHUNG DECIDES

WENTWORTH SLIPPED swiftly into the dark hallway that opened before him. If it had been dark in the alley outside, it was even darker here. In the pitch blackness he could see nothing at all. But he could hear the clamor of the mob scrambling over the ash barrels, racing after him, thirsting for his blood. The shouts and the yells of fury assailed his cars for a moment, then they were shut out with the quick, noiseless closing of the door. In a moment Wentworth felt as if he had been transplanted to a different land. The sudden surcease from the relentless pursuit, from the nerve-racking action of the past few minutes, left him weary, exhausted.

He leaned against the wall of the narrow hallway in the pitch blackness, and listened to the sounds of the frenzied search for him in the alley, to the sudden shouts of frustration and rage. "He's escaped! The Spider's escaped. It's a blind alley. He must be in here yet—that door! He must have gone through there. Break it down!" Blows began to rain upon the door, and the timbers buckled under the assault.

In the darkness, Wentworth felt the presence of the person who had admitted him. As his eyes grew accustomed to the blackness, he made out a thin, darkly-garbed figure beside him, heard a sibilant, singsong whisper:

"So the Spider flees. And be comes to Wang Chung for sanctuary! Come. Wang Chung awaits you. He gave word to admit you if you should come."

Wentworth spoke swiftly: "Hurry. The door will give in a second!"

"Put your hand on my shoulder, and follow me carefully!"

He followed the man along the narrow hallway until they came to a doorway giving on another street. The guide peered out carefully, and drew back with a jerk as he saw a police radio car dash into the block. He crowded back against Wentworth, muttering in a singsong dialect. Behind them, the alley door was splintering under the blows of the attackers. The radio car

PRINCESS ISSORIS

KHANDRA VEG

WANG CHUNG

sped past the doorway, and rounded the corner, evidently going to the scene of the chase. The street was clear. The guide grunted, and darted out, with Wentworth close behind him. Back of them there was a crash, and the door gave. The pursuing mob jammed into the hallway.

But Wentworth and his guide had already run down the street, stepped into another hallway. In silence they ascended a flight of stairs, a second and third, and climbed out on to a roof. They crossed three roofs, then descended through a skylight into a basement, while outside in the street, police whistles shrilled and sirens screamed.

The guide said nothing, leading the way in silence, through the basement into a coal bin. There was a low door in the rear wall of the bin, leading into a narrow passageway that sloped downward. Wentworth and his guide had to bend over almost double to traverse this passage. From the angle, Wentworth judged that it led under the street, to the opposite side. He was right. It sloped up once more, brought them into another basement. They climbed a rickety flight of stairs, and the guide rapped on a door. It was immediately opened by a short, stocky Chinese, who wore horn-rimmed glasses.

The guide bowed low, spoke in Cantonese, which Wentworth understood very well. "O Wang Chung, the Spider came to the door of escape, as you foretold, and I have brought him here. They search for him everywhere in the streets."

Wang Chung nodded curtly to the guide, and stood aside for Wentworth to enter. He said, speaking in faultless

TANG - AKHMUT

MARCIA GRANT

DARWIN GRANT

English, with only the slightest hint of a lisp: "You are welcome, Spider, if you come in peace. I owe you a debt, which tonight I can pay. I hoped that you would come here for sanctuary, when I heard on the radio that you were being sought throughout the city."

Wentworth stepped in, and Wang Chung closed the door, leaving the guide on the outside. "Tonight," he said slowly, "I come in peace, Wang Chung. I am hard-pressed, and I need sanctuary—and help!"

The stocky Chinaman smiled. His long saffron face was inscrutable and his narrow eyes studied Wentworth carefully. He was dressed in an ordinary business suit, but instead of a coat he wore a beautiful white silk jacket over his vest. His black hair was close-cropped, and his forehead was high, narrow.

THE ROOM was very large, with a costly, soft rug on the floor, and teakwood furniture tastefully arranged. Against one wall there was a tall bookcase, crammed full of books. In a corner, near a second door, there was a wrought iron stand upon which rested a bronze bowl from which rose a gentle curling plume of incense smoke. The strange, sweet odor filled the room, permeated soothingly to Wentworth's nostrils.

Wang Chung motioned Wentworth to a chair, handed him a box of cigars from a desk in the center of the room. Wentworth refused. He raised his eyes to the stocky Chinaman, said baldly:

"Wang Chung, the whole city is looking for the Spider. There is a reward of one hundred thousand dollars to the man who turns in the Spider, dead or alive. Frankly, I know that you are a criminal, a racketeer. You have smuggled in hundreds of your countrymen, hatchet men from the Northern provinces whom you use to terrorize small Chinese business men throughout the country into paying tribute to you.

"Once in the past the Spider did you a small service. Twice in the past the Spider broke up certain activities of yours. Today, the Spider needs help, and remembers that on the occasion when he did you that small service, you took an oath to repay it. Do you still consider that the oath holds good—in spite of the other things the Spider has done? Or does the hundred thousand dollars tempt you?"

While Wentworth spoke, Wang Chung had listened attentively. Dimly, as if from a great distance, they heard the sounds of police sirens. They were coming from the street, but the walls of this house in Chinatown were soundproof. For a long minute, Wang Chung stood facing Wentworth without answering. Then he stepped back a pace, his face still impassive, and clapped his hands twice. Almost instantly, the door in the opposite wall opened, and a young Chinese woman appeared. She was attired in the flowered garments of the East, with her hair done high on her head. Her features, small and regular, formed a delicate oval of fragile beauty. There was a high intelligence in her youthful face, and she advanced diffidently into the center of the room, looking affectionately at Wang Chung.

The Chinaman spoke to her softly in Cantonese: "Li Chi, Flower of my heart, look upon the man who sits here. You have seen him once before. His face is changed, for he has used the skillful art of the actor. But he it is who is known as the Spider!"

The girl's face lit up with a happy smile. She glanced shyly at

Wang Chung, then stepped forward
and knelt beside Wentworth, took his
hand in both of hers, and pressed it to
her forehead, then to her breast. She
spoke with a lilting singsong that was
sweet to the ear, in Cantonese:

"O man who is known as the
Spider, I name you every day when
I pray to our venerable ancestors. My
head and my heart are always filled with gratitude toward you
for the thing that you once did!"

Wentworth smiled, arose, and raised her to her feet. "I am
glad that you think so well of me, Li Chi, and I am happy that
you commend me to your revered ancestors."

Li Chi curtsied gracefully, and backed out of the room. "Later,
when you have finished your business with my honorable lord,
I will bring tea," she said.

When she had left the room, Wang Chung turned to Wentworth. His face was still the saffron mask of the east, but there
was a gleam in his narrow eyes.

"You asked me a question, Spider," he said in English. "You
shall have your answer!" He came up close to Wentworth, spoke
with a sudden unexpected gush of feeling. "My wife, Li Chi, is
the dearest thing in the world to me. Some years ago, when I
sent for her from China, she landed at midnight, from a boat
on the San Francisco waterfront. Enemies of mine seized her,
would have killed her.

"It was then that a man known as the Spider stood between

those enemies and Li Chi, with two blaring guns in his hands. At the risk of his own life, he saved Li Chi." Wang Chung blinked, went on huskily. "You speak of one hundred thousand dollars, Spider. It is much money. But if it were all the gold in the world, Spider, it would not tempt me now—now that I have the chance to repay to you the debt which I owe!"

"Even"—Wentworth spoke slowly—"if I should ask you for help against Tang-akhmut. The Man from the East?"

"Even that, Spider. Tang-akhmut is very powerful—so powerful that you have failed against him twice. He controls the police here in the city, and he has a strange hold on the people. You see how he has enraged them against you. I cannot understand his power—yet I will help you to fight him. In that, I am not selfish. For Tang-akhmut will destroy me if he can. He has decreed that there shall be no power in the city other than his!"

"I see," Wentworth said meditatively. "I suppose he's approached you?"

Wang Chung nodded. "His emissary was here today. Khandra Veg. I must pay half of my earnings to Tang-akhmut, or there will be no mercy for me!"

"Then I propose an alliance, Wang Chung. You and I have always been on opposite sides. It has been your business to break the law, mine to uphold it. Now, while the common enemy threatens, we will be allies. I need you, Wang Chung"—Wentworth's face had become haggard under the make-up—"because one whom I love even as well as you love Li Chi, is in the hands of The Man from the East.

"And I, the Spider, am stripped of my wealth and my friends

and my resources. You have hundreds of hatchet men through-out the country, and you have much wealth. You must throw all of that into the alliance. I, on the other hand, have nothing to offer but the brain and the guns of the Spider."

The eyes of the stocky Chinaman met those of Richard Went-worth. "It is well," Wang Chung said softly.

And the two men shook hands.

IT WAS at this moment that a respectful knock sounded on the door, and a servant entered. He was not an ordinary servant. Pock-marked, with a long ugly scar on the right side of his neck, he carried himself more with the assurance of a fighting man than of a servitor. Wentworth knew that this was one of the two hundred-odd hatchet men who obeyed Wang Chung. There was a bulge under his shoulder, and there would also be, Went-worth was aware, a smooth sheath somewhere on him, with a keen knife that he could probably throw with greater accuracy than most men can shoot.

Wang Chung said to him: "What is it, Lee?"

"Honorable Leader," Lee replied in the singsong Cantonese, "the one you expect is here—Bart Peyton, the evil one."

Wentworth glanced quickly at Wang Chung. He recognized the name of Bart Peyton. Peyton had long been the city's over-lord of the vice and drug traffic. The man was unscrupulous, merciless. Since the advent of Tang-akhmut, however, he had drawn in his tentacles, had lain low, fearful of the greater crim-inal who had come to usurp the field.

Wang Chung explained, making a grimace of distaste: "Peyton is a very disgusting person, and a dangerous man. I despise his sort, but I agreed to let him come here. We were to talk about Tang-akhmut. You see, The Man from the East has also given Peyton an ultimatum—he may operate as before, provided he pays fifty percent to Tang-akhmut. Peyton and I were to decide whether to bow to Tang-akhmut or defy him. Perhaps you would rather wait in another room?"

"No!" Wentworth decided at once. "Let him come in. If we are to fight Tang-akhmut, we shall need all the allies we can get—even men like Peyton!"

Wang Chung shrugged. "I warn you, that he will knife you in the back at the first chance."

He stopped at the slow smile on Wentworth's face. "We will try not to give him the chance, Wang Chung!"

"Very well, Spider." He motioned to the hatchet man. "Bring in the man, Peyton!"

Bart Peyton was the type of man whose character is stamped upon his face. Broad-nosed, thick-lipped, with almost colorless eyes placed close together, he swaggered into the room. He was dressed meticulously, in a tight-waisted gray suit, with a blue shirt and tie to match, and a blue-bordered handkerchief in his breast pocket. He stared insolently at Wentworth, without recognizing him, then said to the Chinaman:

"I thought this was gonna be a private talk, Wang Chung." He flicked a thumb at Wentworth. "Who's this gent?"

Wang Chung smiled placatingly. "He is my friend and ally, Peyton. He, too, is interested in fighting Tang-akhmut. Perhaps we three—"

Peyton held up a broad hand. "Nix! If you think you can stand up to the Egyptian, it's your funeral. Me, I'm gonna give in. Tang-akhmut has enough on me to send me to the chair. As long as he holds that stuff, I'm his man. And believe you me, mister, there's plenty more men in this town would like to know where he keeps his private papers!"

Wentworth met Peyton's glance. "Suppose I were to tell you, Peyton, that Tang-akhmut's authority is about to be challenged. Suppose I were to tell you that The Man from the East may not remain the king-pin for long?"

Peyton laughed scornfully. "Then I'd tell you you were nuts, mister! You don't know the situation in the city. Why, Tang-akhmut holds the whole police force. The only reason I come here is because he told me to see could I get Wang Chung to fall in line. Why, I opened up all my joints tonight. I got twenty clip joints in the city, an' they're all running strong, an' not a cop comes near them. The saps get taken, an' they go out an' squawk, an' the cops tell 'em to go sit on a tack! How's that, boy? I give half to Tang-akhmut, but that's better than goin' to the chair!"

Wentworth tried another tack. "You can't be all bad, Peyton, though you make a living in a vicious way. But do you want to see the whole city in the power of a beast like Tang-akhmut?"

"Lay off!" Peyton growled. "You talk like a preacher!" His eyes narrowed, and he swung on Wang Chung. "Look here. Chink! What you tryin' to pull on me? Who's this guy, anyway?"

"I," Wentworth said slowly, "am the man who is going to fight Tang-akhmut to a standstill." He came up close to the other. "Can you guess who I am?"

FOR A moment Peyton gazed at him defiantly. Then the things that he saw in Wentworth's eyes made his jaw sag. "You—Gawd, you can't be—the Spider!"

Wentworth nodded grimly. "The Spider is willing now to overlook your vicious criminal record. The Spider offers you an alliance. An alliance to rid the city of Tang-akhmut. What do you say, Peyton?"

The other gulped. His glance rested fearfully on the Spider's empty hands—hands which had so often held guns that had dealt death to men whom Peyton had known. "I—I can't, Spider," he beamed. "That Egyptian would release the stuff he's holding against me Nobody can buck Tang-akhmut—not even you! Look how they're chasin' you."

He went to the window, pulled up the blind. Downstairs, in Pell Street, radio cars were pulled up at the opposite curb. Police with sawed-off shot guns and tear gas bombs were moving up and down. They had thrown a cordon about the block across the street, and they were going through it with a fine-toothed comb.

"See that?" said Peyton. "How can you buck all that? You said in that letter that you would rob the Finney Finance Company tonight. Everybody knows that the Finney Company is Tang-akhmut's outfit. They say that's where they keep all the blackmail stuff that makes everybody fall in line. And there's lots of guys hopin' that you'll pull it off. But you couldn't get within a block of the Finney Company tonight. You'd be walkin' into a bloody trap. You're hog-tied, Spider. Personally, I'd like to see you put it over." He shook his head. "But it can't be done!"

Wentworth gazed down into the street speculatively. "What if I were to rob the Finney Company tonight? What if I were to get possession of all those papers—including the ones that implicate you?"

"By God!" said Peyton, "if you did that, I'd tie up with you. But I'd like to lay you a bet of five to two that you couldn't do it. Only"—he added regretfully—"I'd never be able to collect, because you'd be as dead as a doornail if you tried it!"

"Give me your word," Wentworth said, "that you won't reveal my hiding place here. Go home and wait for news. In the morning you will hear that the Finney Finance Company has been robbed!"

"You mean to say, Spider," Peyton demanded suspiciously, "that you're gonna break the law—that you're gonna *rob* this place? What's the idea of pullin' a stunt like that, anyway?"

"I'll tell you why. As you say, the police are somehow under

NITA VAN SLOAN

the thumb of Tang-akhmut. My friend, Kirkpatrick, the police commissioner, is in jail on a trumped-up charge of murder, and Deputy-Commissioner Grant seems to be playing into the hands of the Man from the East. Therefore, I am going to organize—shall we call it a mob of my own?

"I'm going to organize the underworld against him. I'm going to prove to the underworld that the Spider can do what he promises. I've promised publicly to rob the Finney Finance Company. Once I carry off the contents of the Finney vaults, everybody will know that The Man from the East no longer has a hold over him. You, and all the others who serve Tang-akhmut through fear, will fall away from him.

"If I succeed, I want you and Wang Chung here, to spread the word in the underworld that it is war to the finish between the Spider and The Man from the East!"

Wentworth turned away from the window, faced Peyton. "When you leave here, you can, of course, go to the police and tell them where I am, and collect the hundred thousand dollar reward if they capture me. Should you do that, Peyton, I give you the word of the Spider that you will die within twenty-four hours; and the Spider's word has never been broken. Now, go. And wait for news tonight!"

Peyton shivered. "I—swear I won't tell the police. I'll wait for news. Could you tell me how you figure to get to the Finney Company through the police and Tang-akhmut's men?"

"You'll know about it in the morning, Peyton!" Wentworth motioned to Wang Chung. "Have Mr. Peyton shown out!"

THE CHINAMAN hesitated, gave Wentworth an appealing look. But Wentworth repeated: "Let him go at once. Call Lee, and have Mr. Peyton shown out!"

Wang Chung shrugged, and reluctantly pressed a button near

the door. In a moment the hatchet man, Lee, entered. Wang said to him in Cantonese: "Take this one out through the side exit, Lee."

Wentworth interrupted, also speaking in Cantonese: "Make some excuse first, Lee, and go out and arrange to have this man followed. His every move must be reported at once!"

Lee glanced to Wang Chung for confirmation. Wang nodded. "Obey him!"

Wentworth switched to English, for Peyton's benefit: "Be sure, Lee, that Mr. Peyton gets away from here without being observed."

Lee bowed. "I go," he said, "to see if street is clean. Come light back. Okay?"

"Okay," Wentworth told him.

Lee stepped out of the room, returned in a few moments. "All light. Mister Peyton, come quick."

Peyton glanced from Wang to Wentworth, said: "Well, so-long. I'll be waiting to hear from you!" There was a queer malicious gleam in his small eyes as he followed the hatchet man out. As soon as he was gone, Wang Chung swung on Wentworth.

"Spider!" he exclaimed. "It was a mistake to let that man go. His promise means nothing. He will go to the police at once. In a few minutes they will turn those machine guns and bombs on us. You have signed your own death warrant—and perhaps my own!"

Wentworth shook his head, smiling. "No, Wang Chung, he won't go to the police. But I hope to God I've guessed him right!"

"What—what do you mean? You don't think he'll keep his promise?"

"I think he will. He has never known the Spider to break a promise, and I promised to kill him if he informed the police. But"—Wentworth paused—"*I said nothing about telling Tang-akhmut where I am!*"

For once, Wang Chang's Chinese stolidity was broken. His face expressed amazed incredulity. "You—you *want* him to tell Tang-akhmut you are here?"

"Exactly. He did not come here to talk things over with you. He came as a spy from Tang-akhmut, to find out whether you intended to play ball. Now he'll go back and report that I'm here. *And I want him to do that!*"

Wang Chung's face was gray. "But that will bring men all down on us. Tang-akhmut will notify the police department—"

"No, he won't. Not if I've sized him up right."

He paused as a knock sounded on the door. Lee the hatchet man entered, bowed, and reported: "I obey the white man's orders, I stationed our men in the street before taking the man, Peyton, out. And he hurried down the street to the Bowery, where a car stands at the curb, with a beautiful woman, and an Egyptian. The Egyptian is Khandra Veg, the one who was here this morning. Peyton spoke to them, and Khandra Veg went quickly to a telephone booth."

Wang Chung nodded. "You have done well, Lee. Yet you give me bad news. Go now, and bring up the men from the cellars. We must prepare to flee."

"No, no!" Wentworth cut in. "There won't be any attack. Just

86

let things ride, Wang Chung. I think I've guessed right!" Reluctantly, Wang Chung nodded to Lee. "Very well. Do nothing. But keep a careful watch—"

"And if Khandra Veg comes," Wentworth broke in, "bring him right up here."

Lee bowed, and went out puzzled. Wang looked quizzically at Wentworth. "I do not understand. Why should Khandra Veg come here? Why should he not at once bring the police?"

"I have told you"—Wentworth's eyes were glowing with suppressed excitement—"that I think that Tang-akhmut holds prisoner one whom I love very dearly. Somewhere in this city is the place which Tang-akhmut has chosen for his headquarters. This person whom he holds prisoner will be there, no doubt. Khandra Veg is probably phoning to his master for instructions. And it is my guess that Tang-akhmut will instruct his servant to come here and give me an ultimatum—"

HE WAS interrupted once more by Lee's discreet rap. Wang called out: "Enter!" and the door opened to admit the hatchet man—with Khandra Veg beside him!

The Egyptian bowed, smiling sardonically. "My master, the Living Pharaoh, sends you his compliments, Spider, on the miraculous way in which you escaped our trap at the bridge tonight!"

Khandra Veg turned smoothly to Wang Chung. "And to you, my master sends this word: he is displeased that you have given refuge to the Spider. My master's displeasure generally means death. But he will be merciful this time. See that you never displease him again!"

Wang Chung's face was again inscrutable. His eyes flicked to the eyes of Lee, the hatchet man, who moved over slightly, so as to be behind Khandra Veg.

Wentworth said softly: "You no doubt also have a message for me, Khandra Veg?"

"Yes, Spider. I could have sent the police in here to capture you. But they would have attacked with guns and gas bombs. You would probably have resisted, and been killed. My master, however, wants you alive. He wishes to—er—speak with you. Therefore, I have come here, to ask you to come with me voluntarily to stand before the Living Pharaoh!"

Wentworth asked, still in his silken voice: "Of course, you can give me a very good reason why I should put myself in the power of Tang-akhmut?"

"Indeed, yes," Khandra Veg told him imperturbably. "You are clever enough to have guessed already, that your fiancée, Miss Van Sloan, is—er—a guest, however unwilling, of my master's. She and a servant of yours by the name of Ram Singh, are at this moment in a certain room, in very uncomfortable circumstances. About their bodies there is a vise, which can be tightened until all the ribs are smashed.

"It is very painful, I assure you. Those vises will surely be tightened all the way unless you come to beg for their lives from my master. Should you come, my master desires me to convey to you his pledge that Miss Van Sloan and Ram Singh will be liberated. That, sir"—Khandra Veg bowed mockingly—"is my message!"

Wang Chung sucked in his breath sharply, glanced at Wentworth, who did not show by the quiver of a muscle in his face that the message had affected him in any way. He said very quietly:

"Thank you, Khandra Veg, for a very concise picture of the situation. And now—*please put your hands up!*"

Magically, there had appeared in his hand one of his guns, pointed unwaveringly at Khandra Veg's chest. Khandra Veg stood still, startled for a moment. Then he grinned defiantly.

"That is a useless and foolish gesture. Spider. However"—he shrugged—"if it pleases you, I will obey." He raised his hands. "You can gain nothing by holding me here. It will not free Miss Van Sloan!"

Wentworth stepped up close to the Egyptian, seized his wrists and twisted them behind him. "Some cord, Wang Chung!" he ordered. In a moment Khandra Veg was securely tied, and Wentworth was issuing swift orders to Lee, the hatchet man, and to Wang Chung.

"The time has come for action! Wang Chung, you will remain here and guard this one. Lee, go down and get together a dozen of your men. Wait for me downstairs!"

WHEN LEE left, Wentworth swiftly stripped off his own clothing. He laid aside the small bundle containing his broad-brimmed hat and cape, which he had stuck in his waist-band. He untied Khandra Veg long enough to remove the Egyptian's tweed jacket and purple tie, and donned them himself.

Then, while Wang Chung watched in amazement, Wentworth knelt beside the helpless Egyptian, and took from his own discarded clothes a folding leather case which he opened to reveal tubes of face pigment, putty, an assortment of small metal plates of various sizes, and a small mirror. Swiftly Wentworth worked with the make-up material, molding it onto his own face, studying Khandra Veg's features as he did so. The Egyptian looked up at him from suddenly hate-filled eyes as he realized what Wentworth was doing.

And under the startled, almost incredulous gaze of Wang Chung, Wentworth's face slowly underwent a subtle change. His cheeks became darker, his forehead appeared to be higher, his chin longer. His straight, patrician nose assumed a slight hook, like that of Khandra Veg's, through the application of a little plastic material. At last, Wentworth regarded the finished job in the glass, sighed with satisfaction, and arose.

Wang Chung gasped. Though Wentworth could not have passed under close scrutiny for the Egyptian, the resemblance was so startling as to be uncanny. Now, Wentworth took a little carmine paint from one of the tubes, smeared it along his left temple, where it lay like a streak of blood.

He looked at Wang Chung, and spoke. And magically, his voice seemed to have changed subtly, to carry the overtones that characterized Khandra Veg's voice. "That, sir," he said, "is my message!"

Wang Chung shuddered. "It is marvelous!" he exclaimed. "I would almost swear that it was the Egyptian who just spoke. Spider, you are a great actor."

"Thanks," Wentworth said dryly. "Now, let's see if I can get away with this elsewhere. Watch this man closely. *He must not escape under any circumstances, Wang Chung!*"

"I hear, Spider. What do you plan to do?"

"I'm going to take a long chance on getting Miss Van Sloan and Ram Singh out of the hands of Tang-akhmut. If I succeed, we'll go after the Finney Finance Company later. If I fail, you better pack your belongings and take Li Chi far away, out of reach of the vengeance of The Man from the East!"

He shook hands with Wang Chung, and hastened downstairs. Lee was waiting for him in the lower hallway, with a close-packed group of a dozen slant-eyed, hard-bitten North-of-China hatchet men. In the dim-lit hallway, Lee stared at him, then uttered a swift oath in Cantonese, and his band flew to his collar, appeared with a gleaming knife.

"Egyptian dog!" he exclaimed. "How did you escape—?"

"Hold it!" Wentworth chuckled. "You see, Lee, you can't always trust your eyes!"

Lee froze, with the knife raised, as the voice of the Spider came from the mouth of the Egyptian, Khandra Veg. He pulled out a flashlight, shone it in Wentworth's face, and muttered softly to himself in Cantonese. Then he said aloud: "Truly, one could swear that you were the Egyptian if one should see you without good light. You are a great magician, Spider! Lead us, and we will follow!"

"Have you got a car?"

"There are two in the garage next door."

"Take your men in both cars, and drive out to the auto in which the woman sits, who awaits Khandra Veg. Is it still there?"

"It is still there, Spider. The woman waits."

"Good. Pull up at a little distance behind. Wherever that car goes, you must follow. If anyone should interfere, the group in one of your cars must eliminate that interference, and leave the other free to follow. Understand?"

"It shall be done, Spider!"

WENTWORTH FOLLOWED them out, waited until they had gone into the garage next door, and until the two cars drove out. Then he walked around the corner, moved toward the car he saw at the curb, where Issoris sat impatiently. Police were moving like shadows through the streets. On the opposite side, a cordon had been thrown about the whole square block, and huddled Chinese stood in groups at the curb while uniformed men went through the houses, inch by inch. A great mob had gathered, and were watching the operations of the uniformed men. Reserves had been called out, and were patrolling the streets, stopping pedestrians and questioning them. Word was being passed from mouth to mouth that the Spider was cornered in that block, and that it was only a matter of time before he would be smoked out.

A long Cadillac limousine, with a police shield on the radiator, pulled up alongside the curb, and a voice hailed Wentworth:

"Say, Khandra Veg!"

Wentworth hastily drew a handkerchief from his pocket, put it up to his face where the blood-like streak of paint marred his forehead. Then he turned toward the limousine. His eyes narrowed as he recognized Acting Police Commissioner Darwin Grant.

Grant was a thin nervous man of fifty, with a wisp of a mustache, and a mole under his left eye. He had been first deputy commissioner, and had succeeded to the command of the police department when Wentworth's friend, Commissioner Kirkpatrick, had been placed in jail on a charge of murder.

Ever since that occasion, the whole police department had seemed to be helpless against Tang-akhmut, even subservient to him. That Grant should know Khandra Veg by sight, that he should hail him openly in the street, was matter for thought for the Spider.

With the handkerchief so arranged that it covered a great part of his face, Wentworth approached the police limousine. "At your service, sir," he said, imitating to perfection the suave, smooth tones of the Egyptian whom he was impersonating.

Grant was alone in the car, except for the uniformed chauffeur. He leaned forward, said excitedly: "I heard about the Spider being here, Khandra Veg. I hope to God they capture him. I came down myself, to make sure they leave no stone unturned."

"They say he is cornered in that block of buildings, sir. It would seem that a mouse couldn't get out of there now."

"Tell me, Khandra Veg," Grant hurried on eagerly. "Your master—is he satisfied with the way everything is going?"

"I—believe so, sir," Wentworth answered cautiously. He was not sure exactly how to act, and he was feeling his way. But inwardly he was tingling with excitement. Here was proof positive that Grant was running the department to please Tang-akhmut. But why? Why should a man like Grant lend himself to the vile plans of the self-styled Living Pharaoh?

"And tell me," Grant demanded almost pitiably, "how—how is Marcia? My daughter, Marcia? She is—well?"

Wentworth's pulse raced. Suddenly the burning force of the

truth thrust itself upon him. He knew Marcia well. As Richard Wentworth, he had often visited at Grant's home, had met the clever, pretty precocious child of sixteen, the only daughter of Deputy Commissioner Darwin Grant. And now Grant was asking Khandra Veg for news of his daughter. The implication was plain, and terrible. Thoughts, plans, raced swiftly through Wentworth's brain.

He answered mechanically: "She is very well sir—very well."

Grant sighed. "That—that is wonderful! She—she talks about me? She asks for me?"

Wentworth studied the piteous, eager face of the father. Abruptly, he came to a decision. "If you will be home tonight, sir, I think I may be able to bring you further news of your daughter."

Grant's eyes suddenly lit up. His thin hand clutched Wentworth's sleeve through the car window. "If—if you would do that! Mrs. Grant is ill in bed. If you could only bring her some good news—a message, perhaps?"

"I shall do my best, sir. Try to be home all night, for I do not know when I shall be able to come."

"I will, I will!" Grant exclaimed fervently. "I'll stay up!"

Wentworth bowed, still holding the handkerchief over his face, and left the acting commissioner, made his way along the street, toward the sedan where Issoris sat. She was beginning to stir impatiently, looking around worriedly. She glimpsed Wentworth approaching, and raised a hand, motioning to him imperiously. She leaned out of the side window, called:

"Hurry, Khandra Veg! What has happened to your face?

What kept you so long?" Wentworth called out: "It is just a scratch. Princess," muffling his voice through the handkerchief.

Now he was taut. He had succeeded in passing as Khandra Veg with the unsuspecting Grant. Would he be as successful with the sharp-eyed, clever Issoris? Everything depended on the next two minutes. With a sidelong glance he saw that the two cars containing Lee and the hatchet men were pulled up behind the sedan in which Issoris rode.

He braced himself, pressed the handkerchief tight against his face, and came up close to the car of the Princess Issoris.

CHAPTER 6
THE DEVIL'S HIGH PRIEST

H E MOVED the handkerchief to one side for a moment, so that she could see the red smear, then quickly covered his face again. The Princess exclaimed petulantly: "You were away a long time, Khandra Veg. Did you find the Spider? And did you deliver my brother's message?"

"I found him, Princess—and he struck me with his gun."

She bit her lip in vexation. "He—refused to give himself up?"

"Yes." Wentworth stood at the door respectfully, with his head averted from the street light. Along the sidewalk, crowds were pressing toward the roped-off area where the search for the Spider was being relentlessly conducted. And even while he answered the princess' questions, there occurred to him the grim irony of the situation: that any one of these hundreds of people who were thronging in to the kill would have turned him over to the police without a qualm—and that his only safety lay in passing himself as the servant of the greatest enemy that these people had!

Issoris was plying him with questions. "Did you tell him that his woman is our prisoner? Did you tell him what will be done to her?"

"I did, Princess. And he struck me!"

Issoris' dark eyes gleamed savagely. "Then we shall make that woman scream with agony! Come! Let us drive back to head-quarters!"

This—this was the moment for which the Spider had planned when he had let Peyton go! He had known that Issoris and Khandra Veg would have followed the pursuit in their car as soon as they got it clear of the cable. He had guessed that Peyton would rather relay the information of the Spider's whereabouts to Tang-akhmut than to the police. And he had counted on posing as Khandra Veg!

He held on to the door, and appeared to reel slightly, as if he were dizzy. "I—I am so sorry, Princess," he said, still muffling his voice with the handkerchief. "I—I am not quite steady, yet, after that blow. If—if you could drive—"

She nodded quickly. "Get in, then!"

His pulse racing, Wentworth got in beside Issoris, who had slipped in under the wheel. In a moment she had snaked the car out from the curb, and was heading out of Chinatown, past the patrols of police, through the milling crowds all seeking a first glimpse of the Spider.

Wentworth threw a swift glance backward after they had

gone a block or so, and glimpsed twin headlights following them steadily. He was satisfied. Wang Chung's hatchet men were on their trail. He sat silently beside the Princess while she drove west across town, then north up the express highway that ran parallel to the New York Central tracks along the Hudson River.

His mind leaped ahead to the things that remained to do that night. Nita must be snatched from the hands of Tang-akhmut, and with her, Ram Singh. The threat he had made to rob the Finney Finance Company must be made good before morning if he was to enlist the support of the city's underworld. True, Peyton had betrayed him. But if the Spider demonstrated that his ingenuity was equal to evading the police and the traps of the Man from the East—which must surely be set at the offices of the Finance Company—then Peyton would come back crawling. And then there was the question of Darwin Grant's daughter, Marcia. From the manner of Grant's query about his daughter, Wentworth guessed that she must also be in the hands of Tang-akhmut.

That theory explained why the police department, under the command of Grant, had appeared to be so subservient to The Man from the East. If Wentworth could manage to release Marcia Grant, then surely her father would no longer fear to proceed against Tang-akhmut.

TAKEN ALONE, each of these feats was a sizeable task. Taken together, they formed a program that would have caused any other man to throw up his hands in despair. But Richard Wentworth had often fought against apparently impossible odds, and had conquered.

Of course, he realized that the day would come when his eternal vigilance, his quickness of judgment and sureness of action, would slip in some small particular and leave him helpless in the face of an enemy. On that day, he knew, he could expect no mercy, but would go down to an ignominious death. Until then, however, the driving impulse within him that had made the Spider a name to be feared and respected in the underworld would urge him on to fight with the last ounce of his energy and brilliant cleverness.

Now, as he sat beside Issoris, he reflected that the events of the night, though they had seemed to move in a helter-skelter phantasmagoria of aimless action, had all led inevitably to this moment when Issoris, the sister of the man who termed himself the Living Pharaoh, should be unknowingly leading the Spider to the lair of Tang-akhmut.

He realized, too, that the dreadful ten minutes he had spent on the roof of that trolley car had not been wasted, for they had led him to the retreat of Wang Chung, and thence into the street where he had been hailed by Darwin Grant. Had it not been for that flight from the mob he would never have learned the secret of Tang-akhmut's hold over the police department.

Wentworth was, above all, a fatalist. So often had he faced death, ruin, extinction, and so often had he come out of the cauldron of danger unscathed, that he had begun to look upon his life as a thing which his body held in trust for some greater power, and which he would be called upon to yield up at the appointed time, and no sooner. If that appointed time should be tonight, then Wentworth would not qail.

"The Spider!" she shrieked, and her long nails clawed his face.

This life that he led was a great adventure, and every moment a new experience. Even at this moment, as he rode with Issoris, he thrilled to the thought that swift action would be thrust upon him within a small space of time. He did not delude himself that he could carry on the disguise of Khandra Veg once they reached the headquarters of Tang-akhmut.

There, it would no doubt be light. He would be subjected to the scrutiny of The Man from the East, whose piercing eyes would discover the imposture at the first glance. Therefore he must act in the very instant of their arrival. What sort of action would be called for, he had no idea.

Always it had been Wentworth's principle never to plan elaborately in advance, for his experience taught him that no man can foresee every detail of the future.

Issoris drove with a certain savage tenseness not unlike the way she did all things. Their headlights bored into the night, showing Wentworth that they were traveling far uptown. The Princess had reached out and flicked on the radio, and the low strains of a dance orchestra from Chicago mingled with the hum of their tires on the concrete. It was well after midnight, and the programs from the Middle West were taking the place of the New York broadcasts.

Wentworth wondered if the Princess' silence ever since they had hit the express highway meant that she had pierced his disguise. Issoris was clever—very clever. Had she guessed that this man who sat beside her was not Khandra Veg, but the Spider? Was she biding her time, and when they arrived at the headquarters of the Living Pharaoh, would she suddenly call for help, denounce him, and turn to laugh insolently in his face, taunting him with his mistake in thinking he had fooled her?

Abruptly, the orchestra music over the radio was replaced by the voice of a late news announcer from Chicago.

"*Inter-radio Press* learns that the mysterious character known as the Spider has succeeded in making good at least one part of his threat tonight. It will be recalled that *Inter-radio* reported exclusively earlier tonight, the contents of the open letter sent by the Spider to the newspapers and the police department of New York, announcing that he would enter the city before midnight, and rob the vaults of the Finney Finance Company before morning.

"Well, the Spider has entered New York! By a clever ruse he evaded the guards stationed at the Williamsburg Bridge, engaged in a running street fight with officers of the law, and disappeared in Chinatown. He is reported cornered in a block in the Chinese section of the city, and his capture may be announced imminently."

THE PRINCESS Issoris exclaimed with a sudden burst of anger: "The fools! Do they expect to capture the Spider there, like a cornered rat? He is too clever for them. He must be out of there long ago! How I hate him, for all his cleverness, Khandra Veg! How I would like to see him squirm under the torture!" She gripped the wheel tight. "I shall satisfy myself by witnessing the death agony of his woman!" She became silent as the radio announcer continued:

"If the Spider succeeds in escaping the cordon, he will have a far more difficult task ahead of him in carrying out the second

101

part of his threat—the robbery of the vaults of the Finney Finance Company. On Fourteenth Street, where the Finance Company is located, the police have planted machine guns at convenient spots commanding the Finney Building. The street is patrolled by a hundred men. The safe itself is guarded by a picked squad under the orders of Inspector Thomas.

"It seems that the Spider has undertaken the impossible. Just what his purpose is, it is hard to say. Those in a position to know hazard the guess that the Spider is throwing down a challenge to the sinister forces that now seem to control the criminal life of the city. It is rumored that a strange man from the East has assumed the overlord-ship of the underworld, ousting the Spider, and that the Spider is staging a come-back."

Wentworth was no longer listening. Issoris had swung into Riverside Drive, and now she was slowing up at the foot of a steep hill leading off the Drive. Looking up toward the top of the hill, Wentworth could perceive some sort of low structure. The Princess brought the car to a complete stop, with the headlights focusing upward toward this building. Risking a quick glance out through the back window, Wentworth caught sight of two cars moving slowly past the side road, proceeding up the Drive at a snail's pace. Those were the cars of Wang Chung's hatchet men. They had stuck to the car!

Wentworth's eyes slid back to Issoris, saw that she was reaching for the headlight button. She clicked off the headlights, then clicked them on, off, and on again. Some sort of signal, of course. From a window in the building on the hill a red light winked twice. Issoris said: "There's the signal. The coast is clear!"

She started the car once more, drove halfway up the dirt road, and stopped once more. The path was blocked by a six-foot-high gate, with barbed wire across the top. A man stepped out from the darkness and came alongside the car. He was a Eurasian of some kind, and he held a carbine in the crook of his arm. The man's eyes gleamed sharply in the darkness, and he bowed low when he saw the Princess.

"Your servant greets you!" he said. "The Living Pharaoh holds late services."

"Open the gate!" Issoris commanded imperiously.

The man stepped back, raised a hand in signal, and someone behind the gate swung it open, leaving the road clear for the car to the top of the hill. Wentworth was watching carefully. Apparently this gate to the stronghold of Tang-akhmut was well guarded. Once he entered here, he would be effectively cut off from the assistance of the hatchet men. Whatever he did, would have to be done by himself alone. The Eurasian's remark about late services interested Wentworth. He sat tensely while Issoris brought the car around into a gravel path, and halted it under a wide *porte-cochère*.

Another Eurasian stepped out from the entrance and held the door open for them. Here it was still dark, and there was little chance for anyone to scrutinize Wentworth's disguise. He helped the Princess out of the car, and followed her into the building. It was an old house, which had been gutted and remodeled. The door opened directly into a large foyer, softly illuminated by an indirect lighting system, Wentworth held himself tightly, hand close to his shoulder holster.

At any moment now, recognition might come, and he would have to fight. But there was no one in the foyer. The Eurasian who had admitted them remained outside. The Princess advanced quickly toward a draped entrance in the far wall, saying carelessly over her shoulder: "Hurry, Khandra Veg. We will be late for the services!"

THEY MOVED through a corridor lined with closed doors, climbed a spiral staircase, and emerged on a small balcony. They were in darkness here, but the room upon which the balcony looked was well lighted. Thirty or forty men and women stood there, hands clasped over their heads, eyes raised to a dais opposite the platform where Wentworth and the Princess stood. Upon that dais stood a single man. He was attired in chased metal mail, which reflected the lights from two dozen tapers, held by Nubians who stood along the walls.

This man's head was not visible, for it was covered by a hideous helmet which was cunningly shaped into the form of a bird's head. The beak was long, curved, dangerous looking. And from within that helmet came the sonorous voice that Wentworth would never forget—the voice of Tang-akhmut, The Man from the East, the man who claimed to be the Living Pharaoh!

Tang-akhmut, attired in the vestments of a priest of ancient Egypt! And he was praying in an ancient Coptic language, which Wentworth identified but could not understand.

The group of worshippers in the room were intent, apparently fascinated by the rite. Their eyes were fixed unwaveringly upon Tank-akhmut, and they kept their hands tightly clasped above their heads. There were half a dozen Eurasians among them, like those *thugs* who had attacked the Spider earlier in the night. But the majority were white, of many types. The seven or eight women showed unmistakable evidences of culture and refinement, and Wentworth thrilled as he identified Marcia Grant among them, the daughter of the acting police commissioner!

Abruptly, Tang-akhmut ceased his weird chant. With the stopping of his voice, there was utter silence for a moment, and then a deep sigh went up from the crowd. They lowered their hands, stood expectantly, still looking up to the dais.

Tang-akhmut spoke once more, but this time in English, apparently for the benefit of the whites: "I, Tang-akhmut, the living Pharaoh, speak to all you true believers! I am he who has read the Book of Thoth, and I know all the secrets of the Gods. I can make those to live again who have died, and I can order the course of events! I am the High Priest of Thoth—"

Wentworth's lips tightened. He understood now what that regalia of Tang-akhmut's meant. That bird-head of his—of course; it was the replica of the ibis-headed god, Thoth, the recorder of all the other Gods! The hideous figure revolted Wentworth, but it seemed to hold all those others spellbound.

The Man from the East went on: "All you who serve faithfully the ancient Gods of Egypt, who know the secrets of Life and Death, and of the Stars, and the Sun, and the Moon; all ye shall be rewarded with eternal life, and shall live on forever, even as I do! Therefore, ye must not hesitate to obey me to the letter, and ye must welcome death rather than try to avoid it, for the sooner that ye shall have died for the first time, the sooner shall ye be made immortal by me!"

And now Wentworth understood the strange power that Tang-akhmut held over his tools. They believed! They *believed* that he was the Living Pharaoh, and they *believed* that if they died in his service he would bring them back to immortal life! No wonder they did not fear to die! No wonder that Khandra Veg had laughed at him when he held the cold muzzle of a gun at his neck!

TANG-AKHMUT'S VOICE possessed a strange magnetism that held his hearers rapt. Even Wentworth felt himself coming under the influence of the droning tones. He glanced sideways at the Princess Issoris, and saw that she was looking down upon the scene with avidly shining eyes, her red lips parted in a curling smile of triumph. And indeed, it was a triumph for Tang-akhmut. Marcia Grant, who was an educated, cultured girl, was as much under the influence of the mystic rites as any of the ignorant Eurasians there.

This strange cult of the East, which held out hope to dispel men's deep-lying fear of death, could very well seize hold upon the Occidental world, could sweep Tang-akhmut to the highest pinnacle of power.

Tang-akhmut was intoning: "So, ye shall obey me to the letter! When I say *kill*, ye shall kill, even if it be a brother or a sister! For the ties of blood are as nothing in the great chasm of time where ye must remain dead if I cast you aside. *Now*—" both hands raised in benediction, Tang-akhmut's gruesome ibis-head turned from side to side—"all ye who place themselves in the keeping of the wisdom of Thoth, *kneel and adore!*"

The group of men and women on the floor, as well as the

Nubians who held the flickering tapers, sank to their knees, and extended their right hands, palm upward, toward the dais.

The Princess Issoris, forgetful of Wentworth, leaned over the balcony, filling her eyes with the sight of these dupes who were placing the free offerings of their lives upon the road which her brother hoped to climb to power. Her breasts were rising and falling swiftly with the intoxication of the scene. And Wentworth, working swiftly, unnoticed behind her, brought out from under his jacket the small parcel of his cape and broad-brimmed hat.

Quickly he slipped them on, drew one of his guns. This was the moment to strike. Never again would he have the opportunity of shooting down this insidious man, who, if unchecked, might wreak havoc with the civilization of the west. Nita must wait, if she were a prisoner; Ram Singh must wait. His duty was clear. He must kill Tang-akhmut here and now, and he must kill him spectacularly, so that these dupes of his could see and spread the word among the thousands of other dupes throughout the city that the Living Pharaoh was dead.

Issoris turned to him, and her eyes widened at sight of the cape and hat. Into them there leaped a sudden hate, mingled with fear. "The Spider!" she shrieked. "The Spider!" And her long, pointed nails clawed for his face.

Wentworth gripped both her hands in his, twisted her arms behind her back. She fought like a wildcat, but she was no match for him. In a moment he had her helpless, quivering in his grip. He wrapped his left arm about her, pressed her to him, imprisoning both her hands in the one of his, in back of her. He could feel her warm body throbbing against his as he looked down into the room below. Issoris' scream had startled them all, and heads were craning upward toward the darkness of the balcony. The ugly ibis-head of Tang-akhmut was also turned toward them, but Tang-akhmut made no move to leave the dais.

Issoris screamed again and again, switching to a Coptic dialect that Wentworth did not understand. She must be warning her brother of the situation, he thought. He tightened the pressure of his arm around her body. Like an iron band his arms pressed the wind out of her, and he thought grimly that the vise about the body of Nita must be far more cruel.

Issoris ceased screaming, gasping for breath. She sagged in his arm, and he held her up, a dead-weight, but he did not relax his grip on her. He smiled grimly. She was playing 'possum, no doubt. If he should ease the pressure of his arm, let go his grip on her wrists, she would turn on him like a pantheress. So he held tight, and stared down into the room, raising his gun and drawing a bead on the ibis-headed figure of Tang-akhmut, the self-styled high priest of Thoth.

He raised his voice, spoke in the tone of the Spider: "Tang-akhmut, you are a fraud and a charlatan! You are no reincarnation of the Living Pharaoh; you are no high priest of Thoth. You are a mortal man, and I shall kill you now to show these poor fools that they have been worshipping a thing of flesh and blood, just like themselves. If you fear death, Tang-akhmut, turn and run. Then these people will know you are not immortal. But if you are what you claim to be, then stand and take it!"

WENTWORTH'S WORDS were shrewdly calculated

to put Tang-akhmut in a spot. If he stood his ground, he would die. If he ran, then all those dupes would lose their faith in him, would spread the word among the others in the city, and the cult of Thoth would be punctured like a toy balloon.

But Tang-akhmut surprised the Spider. A strange, metallic laugh emanated from the beaked ibis-head. Then, while all the disciples knelt, too petrified to get to their feet, Tang-akhmut spoke out of the recesses of his helmet: "Greetings, Spider! I did not expect you here. It seems you are brave and clever. But the coarse, brutal brand of cleverness of the West is no match for the power of the gods. Shoot, Spider! I welcome this test! If your gun can prevail against the high priest of Thoth, then there is no hope for mortal man. *Shoot!*"

And he stood there, defiant, the curved beak of his ibis-head turned upward toward the balcony. A deep sigh of suspense went up from the assemblage. Wentworth held his automatic steady in his right hand, while his right arm clamped tightly about the soft body of Issoris. He had expected some form of resistance, had at least expected Tang-akhmut to call for help, to attempt to escape. Now his scheme to discredit the Living Pharaoh had boomeranged against him. Wentworth had never in his life shot down a defenseless man. Now he must shoot one who stood apparently defenseless, and unafraid.

He steeled himself. This man was made of the very essence of evil. To let him live through any false sense of sportsmanship was unthinkable. This was not a killing—it was an execution. For the sake of society, for the sake of those poor dupes down below, for the sake of the lives of citizens throughout the city, Tang-akhmut must die!

Deliberately Wentworth steadied the gun at arm's length, so that the sight centered just below the heart. He could have thrown a snap shot with as much accuracy, but he wanted to be sure—*sure*.

He pulled the trigger!

There was a flash of flame, a thunderous report that boomed in the vaulted room. The figure of Tang-akhmut was hurled backward against the drapes behind the dais. He staggered, clutching at the curtains for support. Then, while a gasp of amazement and happiness rose from the devotees on the floor, Tang-akhmut slowly pulled himself erect, stood, unhurt upon the dais. And out of the ibis-head there came a brittle, metallic laughter!

A great shout arose from the disciples. They had seen a miracle with their own eyes! Bitterly, the thought flashed through Wentworth's mind that the glittering mail worn by Tang-akhmut was not only for costume effect; it was for protection. That mail must be bullet-proof material.

Cunningly, The Man from the East had rendered himself invulnerable to bullets while he officiated at the ceremony. And Wentworth's act had only served to strengthen the delusion of these fools that the Living Pharaoh was immortal!

The noise on the floor below was almost deafening. But above it rose Tang-akhmut's commanding voice: "Put out the tapers! The Spider is on the balcony! Capture him! Capture him!"

At once the Nubians doused the candles, and the entire room

was plunged into blackness. In the grim quiet there was the sound of swiftly moving feet. Behind him, on the staircase, Wentworth heard movement, silent, ominous, deadly. He swung about, still supporting Issoris. For a moment his grip on her hands relaxed, and she twisted free, clawed at him wildly. Dark bodies swarmed into the balcony, surrounded them. And Issoris shouted:

"Here he is! Kill him! Kill him!"

CHAPTER 7
"WELL DONE, MASTER!"

WENTWORTH STRUCK out with both fists, a gun now gripped in each. He felt the impact of the cold metal against lithe bodies, heard men drop before his blows. But others came, piling in from the stairs. Hot breath fanned his cheek, and a knife slithered against a gun butt, another bit into his forearm.

A slungshot missed his head by a hair's-breadth, and hit his shoulder a glancing blow as he twisted in the threshing mêlée. His arms worked like pistons, in and out, smashing blows at his attackers with the swift methodical efficiency of the high-powered fighting machine which he was.

He had no need to watch his blows, for he knew that everybody was an enemy. The darkness was now his friend. These attackers were little men, probably *thugs* of the same race as those who had sought to strangle him at the landing field. As he fought, Wentworth kept his neck hunched into his shoulder for fear of another of those deadly loops of wire. But they were too close-packed for such work. Hoarse shouts filled the air, together with the grunts of fighting men and the moans of several who lay on the floor.

Suddenly a pair of wiry arms gripped Wentworth about the ankles, pulled hard. He went over, catching at the railing for balance. A shout of triumph went up from the little men swarming on him, and they threw themselves at him. Wentworth twisted away, slashed downward with one of his guns, felt the muzzle strike hard bone.

There was a wail of pain, and the grip on his ankles was released. He fell on a threshing form, with a pile of men on top of him. Blows rained upon him, on his head, his shoulders, his arms. A heel slashed against his temple, and left a gash there. A knife bit into his thigh. In a moment he would be overwhelmed by the mere weight of numbers.

And above it all, the voice of the Princess Issoris rose in a hate-filled litany: "Kill him! Kill him! *Kill him!*"

Desperately, Wentworth thrust both hands upward into the flailing mass of wiry men, and fired both guns again and again. Slugs thudded into flesh and thunder filled the room, deafening him. Bodies fell away from him. For an instant he was free. And simultaneously, brilliant electric lights sprang up in the ceiling. The room was illuminated clearly, brightly, mercilessly. He saw men threshing about him, wounded; men lying on the floor, stunned; others pressing into the doorway, with knives and guns. Now they could see him, they could shoot!

Wentworth heaved himself up, pistoned his arms in quick

blows that opened a way for him to the railing. A slug whined by his head from the doorway of the balcony, and he snapped a shot at the one who had fired. The man screamed, and reeled backward against the others in the doorway.

A small, wiry *thug* came up from the floor, swinging a glittering knife up in a flashing arc that would have disemboweled the Spider. Wentworth's guns swished down, caught the blade and struck it from the man's hand. More slugs were whistling past him, and the room was filled with gunfire and with shouts.

Wentworth put a leg over the balcony, then the other, and leaped through the air. The balcony was perhaps fifteen feet above the floor, and he landed on his feet. He did not stop, but shot like a plummet for the open door behind the dais. The disciples were still pushing out through the door to get at the staircase, while the women among them were huddled against the wall alongside the dais. Some of the *thugs* were leaping from the balcony after him, and bullets were pitting the floor where he had been.

He glimpsed the white face of Marcia Grant among the women, and as he passed he put out a hand, gripped her white arm, and dragged her with him. She screamed, kicked, but his frenzied strength was irresistible. In a second he had sped through the doorway, kicked it shut just as an avalanche of the small wiry men thudded against it. He slipped home the bolt, and leaned against the door, grinning into the face of the frightened Marcia Grant.

She shrank from him, her lips trembling with fear and loathing. She was young, frail-looking, with a skin of a soft, delicate texture. It was easy to see how one of her susceptible temperament had fallen under the influence of the powerful personality of Tang-akhmut, coupled with the hope of immortality which he held out to his dupes.

WENTWORTH HEARD the pounding on the door behind him, heard the shouts of baffled rage from the other room. He gripped the girl's arm tightly, demanded in a taut voice: "Where did Tang-akhmut go?"

He had not seen The Man from the East when he leaped from the balcony. The Living Pharaoh had apparently not stayed for the outcome of the fight.

Marcia Grant did not struggle against his grip. In a small, frightened voice she said: "I—I don't know. P-please let me go. I—I'm awfully afraid. The Living Pharaoh will destroy you. I—"

There was no time for more. A shot sounded on the other side, and a bullet ploughed through the thick wood just to the left of Wentworth. He grunted: "Come on, Miss Grant!"

He dragged her down the corridor, which opened into another large room. She came reluctantly, but she did not attempt to get away from him. She had heard enough about the Spider to convince her that struggle would be futile. In this, the unfounded tales of ruthlessness and murder which had been spread about him served him in good stead. It enforced the girl's obedience through fear.

In the room which they now entered, there was no sign of anyone. But the walls—all four of them—were lined with racks upon which hung modern, high-powered rifles, automatics, sub-machine guns, tear-gas bombs and grenades. Wentworth whistled as he inspected the array of weapons. This was indeed an arsenal to be proud of. Here were enough weapons to supply all the devotees of Tang-akhmut when he incited them to murder and riot. On the floor there were cases of ammunition, and unopened cases of more rifles, piled to the ceiling.

Wentworth realized that this supply was sufficient to equip enough men to take the city. Tang-akhmut's plan must be far more ambitious than even the Spider had suspected. The Man from the East must be planning a coup which would give him armed control of the city!

And from that, what might he not attempt further? With thousands of duped disciples who did not fear death, he might be strong enough even to march upon the nation's capitol. The reins of government had been seized in many countries already by men of far less personality than Tang-akhmut.

There was a crash in the corridor behind them. The door had been broken down. In a moment the pursuers would be upon them. Wentworth ran to the door by which they had come in, slammed it shut, and locked it. Marcia Grant stood still among the cases of weapons and ammunition, too dazed to try to escape.

She watched, quivering, while Wentworth picked up several small grenades and stuffed them in his pocket. In a special rack he found a load of Mills bombs, and he also took some of these.

He saw her watching him, and said grimly: "Now, Miss Grant, we're going to try and get a couple of friends of mine out of here, and then I'm taking you to your father. I hope he gives you the spanking of your life!"

Wentworth stood rigid there while the autogiro melted into the darkness above.

The devotees were firing through the door of the arsenal room now, and Wentworth seized her arm once more. "We better get out of this room quick! If they should hit some of this ammunition, even your Living Pharaoh wouldn't be able to put together your pieces!"

Marcia Grant stared at him wonderingly, following with passive obedience. This Spider, strangely, did not seem to be such a terrifying person as she had imagined from the stories that were circulated about him. As they ran through the passage leading from the arsenal room, she began to lose her terror, to feel a certain sympathy for him, to wonder who the friends were that he wanted to rescue.

EVEN BENEATH the cape and hat of the Spider, Wentworth had the unusual faculty of making his engaging personality stand out when he wanted it to. To such an extent did he succeed in the few perilous seconds of flight from the killers of Tang-akhmut, that when Marcia glimpsed a group of them far down the hall, blocking their progress, she exclaimed in genuine alarm: "Look! They'll get you!"

Wentworth laughed grimly. "Not now, Miss Grant!"

The *thugs* came running at him down the long corridor, knives flashing in the dim light from the small bulb overhead. He could see their teeth gleaming, their eyes glinting with lust for murder. A few had guns, and shot after shot echoed in the narrow space.

Wentworth pushed Marcia Grant behind him, somehow taking it for granted that she would not attempt to escape any more. Suddenly his guns appeared as if by some mystic legerdemain, spouting fire at the wiry little men. Like things of mechanical precision those two automatics in the hands of the Spider spat death at the attacking group. He fired coolly, carefully, with deadly accuracy.

Once more the Spider's blazing guns were thundering their message of destruction to the forces of evil; a single man against a dozen. Yet that man was the Spider. Behind them, many were coming to take him in the rear. In a matter of seconds that armory door would be down, and Wentworth would be caught between two fires, with nowhere to retreat.

But that thought scarcely entered his mind as he exchanged shots with the bloodthirsty pack in front. Two, three, four, were down. And still his guns blazed, still he fired slowly, surely. All at once, the attackers broke before that withering stream of lead. They turned tail and fled. All Tang-akhmut's power, all his eloquence, all their belief that he was the Living Pharaoh and that by his secret knowledge of the Book of Thoth he could bring them back to life—all that was dissipated by the sight of their dead comrades, and by the wicked, accurate, spitting automatics of the Spider, the man who stood there coolly like a machine and faced them with blazing eyes and blazing guns!

In a moment the hallway ahead was cleared of living foes. Wentworth seized Marcia Grant's hand, urged her forward. Behind them a crashing, splintering sound told them that the second door had yielded to the onslaught of the pursuers. Wentworth raced ahead, catching fleeting glimpses of the fleeing *thugs*. They disappeared down a stairway at the end of the hall, and one of them paused at the head of the stairs, shielding himself behind a door, and raised a knife to hurl at Wentworth.

These men were experts, and the knife would find a sure mark in the Spider's throat. Wentworth snapped a shot at the man's arm, the only part of him exposed, and hit the wrist. There was a squeal of pain, the knife slithered to the floor, and the man screamed again and again as he lost his balance and went hurtling down the steps.

Wentworth, with Marcia Grant behind him, raced for those stairs, hoping to get down them before the pursuers from the arsenal room caught up with them. But a hail of lead arose from down below, drove them back. The hallway was now reverberating with the thunderous denotations of dozens of guns, each new explosion slapping against their ears with paralyzing force. And mingled with the sounds of shooting, came the shouts of the first of the pursuers, who had broken through the door of the arsenal room. They had sighted Wentworth and Marcia.

Tight-lipped, Wentworth dragged the girl after him, past the stair head, down toward the end of the hallway. Shots followed them, and Wentworth snapped a single slug up at the electric light bulb overhead. It disintegrated, splattering glass, and the hall was plunged in darkness.

The men behind shouted, firing as they came after them, and Wentworth pulled the girl toward one side, felt for the knob of a small door he had glimpsed in the outer wall of the corridor just before he shot out the light. He pushed it open, slipped out, shoving Marcia out ahead of him. He closed the door just as the first of the pursuers rushed through the corridor, past the door.

Cold night air greeted them here. They were on the outside, in some sort of garden. Light poured from many windows in the house, showing Wentworth the shadowy figures of men running in the darkness, away from the house, down the hill toward the gate on the road. One of these passed quite close, and mistaking Wentworth for an inmate of the house, called out: "Come quickly! We are attacked at the gate! The Master orders all men to the gate!"

THE MAN was gone, and Wentworth now heard the sounds of gunfire from the direction of the road. Marcia Grant clung to him now, all her fear of him gone. "W-what is happening?"

He grinned in the dark. "Some of my friends, I think, are raiding the place. You know, Miss Grant," he added almost irrelevantly, "the Chinese are a very smart people!"

He took her arm, started to run around the house, peering in at each of the lighted windows. Many of the rooms were equipped as dormitories, with rows and rows of bunks; another was a huge dining room. Wentworth let go of Marcia's arm for long enough to load two clips in his automatics. While he did so, Marcia Grant said timidly: "Aren't you afraid—that I'll try to escape from your—"

He shook his head. "If I'm any judge, you were under some sort of hypnotic spell back there. And I can also see that the spell is broken. You no longer think that Tang-akhmut is the Living Pharaoh, do you?"

She shuddered, following him around the side of the house, while other figures ran past them in the dark toward the gate. The shooting down there had increased in volume. Two men passed them, each with a sub-machine gun under his arm.

"I—I don't know what to think, any more. I only know that if you're the Spider, you're not as fearful a person as I thought—"

She stopped as Wentworth gripped her shoulder. They had just passed a small barred window, opening into a room below the level of the ground. Peering through the bars, Wentworth's face assumed grim, hard lines. He was looking almost directly into the eyes of Nita van Sloan!

Nita's wrists and ankles were still bound to the two pillars, and the cruel vise was clamped tight about her body, just as Khandra Veg had described. A tall Nubian was turning the handle of the vise, playfully, and Nita was holding her little head erect, proudly, not glancing at the man. The clamps of the vise were bearing cruelly against her ribs. The Nubian finished the turn of the handle, and grinned wickedly, licked his lips.

Wentworth's face flushed a deep red. His eyes swiftly traveled over the room, glimpsed Ram Singh, similarly bound. He felt the warm body of Marcia Grant pressing against him, shuddering. "W-who are those poor things?" she asked, raising her voice to make herself heard above the rifle fire and the drumming of the machine guns from the direction of the road.

Wentworth told her grimly: "The people I'm going to rescue. That's the way your friend, Tang-akhmut treats his enemies!"

Marcia shivered. "And I—thought him so wonderful! I—left my father to—come here. W-what a little fool I was!"

Wentworth did not answer. The Nubian was bending over to take another twist in Nita's vise. Wentworth raised a gun, fired into the room through the bars. Window glass crashed, and the Nubian jumped and doubled over with a shriek, pawing with his left hand at the bubbling blood spurting from his broken right arm.

Nita and Ram Singh raised suddenly hopeful eyes toward the window. Two other Nubians in the room drew guns, fired hurriedly, but Wentworth had drawn back with Marcia. "Those bars!" Marcia Grant cried. "You—can't get through them!"

Wentworth was pulling a grenade out of his pocket. Face hard, hands working swiftly; he pulled the pin and threw the grenade so that it landed in the grass just under the Window. Then he dragged Marcia to the ground. There was a crashing, deafening explosion. Bits of mortar and iron fell around them. Before the rolling crash of the explosion had died down, Wentworth was on his feet, racing toward the window. Part of the wall was demolished, and the bars of the window hung in twisted bits, leaving the opening free. He glimpsed Nita, head raised, eyes sparkling, and started to climb through.

ONE OF the Nubians raised a gun to fire at him, and Wentworth shot the man through the head. Ram Singh's voice, tight with warning, reached him above the gunfire from outside: "Watch out Master! The door!"

Another Nubian crouching in the doorway had a knife raised to hurl. Wentworth fired just as the knife left the man's hand. The man was hurled backward through the doorway by the impact of the bullet, and the knife swished past Wentworth's head into the darkness outside.

Ram Singh called out: "Well done, master! Come quickly and release us before others come!" Wentworth climbed in, ran to Nita Van Sloan. She was holding herself erect by sheer power of will. "Darling!" she smiled. "I—didn't—think you could—make it—this time!" And she fainted.

Wentworth grimly reversed the vise, and the clamps spread, leaving wide red welts on Nita's soft skin. Wentworth picked up a knife from the floor, slashed at the bonds that held her ankles and wrists, and eased her limp body gently onto the floor. Then he hurried to Ram Singh and released him. The Sikh had had much more punishment than Nita, and it was easy to see that he was at the end of his tether. Nevertheless he showed his gleaming teeth in a broad smile and tottered over to the dead body of the Nubian, where he picked up the man's gun. "Let us go, master! We will show them how to fight!" he said.

Wentworth gripped Ram Singh's hand for a fleeting instant. The corners of his mouth twitched with sympathy for the effort the Sikh was making to hide the agony of his crushed ribs.

"Good man, Ram Singh!" he said huskily. Then he stooped swiftly, picked up Nita's unconscious body, and motioned for Ram Singh to climb out first. Then he handed Nita out to him, climbed through himself.

Marcia Grant was waiting for them, and she exclaimed: "Poor girl! She's fainted!"

"I have not!" Nita suddenly said, and pushed out of Wentworth's arms, to her feet. She shivered in the cold of the night, abruptly realized that she was unclothed, and blushed. Wentworth took off his cape and wrapped it around her. Then the four of them swiftly ran down toward the road, where the shooting was still lively, toward the rear of those who were defending the gate in the road.

In a few swift words Wentworth explained to Nita and Ram Singh how he had come there. "Those are the hatchet men of Wang Chung," he finished, "who are working with me. They attacked a little too soon, and I'm afraid they'll be overwhelmed if we don't do something about it!" He handed Ram Singh the grenades from his pocket.

"Rear attack, Ram Singh!" he ordered. "Drop those where they'll do the most good. Spot the machine gunners, and clean them up first."

The Sikh grinned. "Orders received, master!" And he began to move forward in the darkness. Wentworth pressed Nita's hand. "Stay here a minute, darling, with Miss Grant. I've a bit of work to do!"

He left them, moving back toward the house. At a respectable distance from the building he halted, eyes narrowed. He took from his pockets two of the Mills bombs he had removed from the arsenal room. True, many of the disciples in there were as innocent as Marcia Grant, and like her, probably under the hypnosis of The Man from the East. But if Tang-akhmut was in there, it was Wentworth's duty to destroy the house, no matter who else perished with him.

He hurled the two Mills bombs.

The resultant explosion made daylight out of the darkness. Garish flames sprang up, accompanied by deafening repercussions. The ground trembled. The walls of the house seemed to be pushed apart by some giant Samson within. Debris hurtled through the air. Fire licked up at the sky. Wentworth watched somberly. He was about to turn away, when he suddenly stiffened, and an oath pressed through his lips.

For from the ground behind the flaming building, a black object rose, ungainly in the night. It was an autogiro, with its revolving vanes swishing through the air with a peculiar humming noise. And in the flaring brilliance of the flames that licked upward from the burning house, two faces peered downward out of the plane—two faces that Wentworth recognized with bitterness. They were Tang-akhmut and his sister, Issoris. **WENTWORTH STOOD** rigid there, while the autogiro melted into the blackness above. The Man from the East was fleeing, leaving his dupes to perish in the flames, to die fighting at the gate in the road. Tang-akhmut was not ready yet to flaunt open defiance of the law. Doubtless he had other places that he could use as headquarters, other dupes and disciples whom he could summon The Living Pharaoh had suffered a defeat at the hands of the Spider. But he could afford it.

At this moment, as Wentworth gazed up into the sky, he felt a strange prescience of the long road of blood and death and misery that lay ahead before the final accounting between the Spider and The Man from the East. He sighed, snapped back into action, and hurried down toward the fighting at the gate. Nita and Marcia Grant fell in behind him as he ran down the road. Here, the complexion of the fighting had changed. Ram Singh met him, grinning, and pointed to a mass of struggling figures. There was no longer a gate there.

"I threw the grenades, master! And the dogs are in the open now. See how the Chinese beat them back! Give me leave, master, to join the fight!" But even as he spoke, a spasm of pain flitted across his face. He put a hand to his side, and slowly slid to the ground. Wentworth knelt beside him anxiously. The Sikh had fainted. Probing, Wentworth found that he had four cracked ribs. Blood dribbled from the Sikh's mouth.

Nita knelt beside him. "Dick! Is he—"

"No, Nita, he's not dead. But he's stood awful punishment." There was pride in the Spider's tone. "He kept on his feet until he'd done his work! What a man!"

Wentworth got to his feet, heaved the heavy body of Ram Singh to his shoulder, and moved down the path toward the fighting. Retainers of Tang-akhmut were streaming past them now, fleeing from the furious onslaught of the Chinese. Ram Singh's grenades had dislodged them from their position, destroyed their machine guns, and at hand-to-hand fighting they were no match for the grim Chinese of Wang Chung.

Lee, the leader of the hatchet men, saw Wentworth and pushed through to him. The yellow man's face was wreathed in smiles. "It was good work, Spider," he said in Cantonese. "The devil-bombs cleared the way for us! Now we will follow these rats and finish—"

Wentworth, gasping under the weight of Ram Singh, broke in: "No, no, Lee. Don't you hear the police sirens? We've got to get out of here fast. Come on. Call your men off!"

He stumbled down the road, with the Sikh on his shoulder, Nita and Marcia trailed after him. He loaded Ram Singh into the car they had left before the gate. Nita took the wheel, backed the auto down the hill. The two front tires were flat, having been hit by rifle fire, and the windshield was scarred by a myriad of tiny cracks from machine gun slugs.

At the foot of the hill they transferred into one of the two cars of the hatchet men. Lee and his men came swarming down, carrying their dead and wounded. In a moment the two cars were racing up the Drive, just as a police radio car sped past them, going toward the scene of the fighting. A little farther up they passed clanging fire engines, which had no difficulty in getting directions to the conflagration, for the flames formed a bright beacon at the top of the hill. But no one stopped them, and in a comparatively short time they were back in the rooms of Wang Chung.

Ram Singh and the wounded Chinese were being treated by a doctor whom Wang had summoned, and who was discreet enough to ask no questions. And in the ornate sitting room, Wentworth was rapidly relating to Wang Chung the events of the night, while Marcia listened in wide-eyed fascination, and Nita Van Sloan helped the dainty Li Chi to serve tea.

WANG CHUNG'S face was impassive as Wentworth finished. "So you see, Wang Chung, I have failed. Tang-akhmut stood before my gun, and I hit him, yet he lives. He lives, and he has many adherents, and much money and power. You have lost a dozen men in tonight's fighting, and if you go on with our alliance I have a much more dangerous mission to undertake tonight. You may lose more men, and bring down on your head the vengeance of Tang-akhmut. There is yet time for you to withdraw—"

Wang Chung shook his head. "I will not withdraw, Spider,"

he said softly. "You say you have failed, but you do not count that you have broken the spell which Tang-akhmut wove over the daughter of Commissioner Grant."

He had switched into Cantonese, so that Marcia started when she heard her name mentioned, but could not understand what was being said. "And you have destroyed a virtual fortress of his. You have rescued the fair lady who is your friend, and also your servant. You are a man of action, and a brave man. I will follow you. If Tang-akhmut is destined to destroy us, so be it. Now, command me. What do you plan for tonight?"

"I'm going to take Miss Grant to her father. Then I shall carry out my plan of raiding the vault of the Finney Finance Company!"

For several minutes he detailed his plans for the night, while Nita swung the dial of the radio set in the corner, seeking to pick up police calls. "First," Wentworth said with a twinkle, "I understand that you do a bit of smuggling occasionally—"

Wang Chung looked at him noncommittally. "Without admitting it, what if I do?"

"Would there be any ship in the harbor at this time that we could make use of as a storeroom for—er—stolen cash and papers?"

"Yes, my friend. The *Orient Queen*, of the China Seas Trading Company, is in the North River now, preparing to clear for Canton tomorrow."

"Good. Now, I happen to know that you have been accused of using bombs, in certain Tong wars that rocked Chinatown some years ago. I do not say that these charges were true, of course, but it would be very convenient if we could find some of those bombs. I heard that they did not explode, but emitted a very dense cloud of smoke, accompanied by flares that resembled flames, but were harmless. There was a story at one time, Wang Chung, that you routed a small army of Mexican hijackers along the border with these harmless bombs."

Wang Chung smiled almost imperceptibly. "You have heard of many queer stories, Spider. I do not say that those stories are true—but I could find you such bombs."

"At once?"

"At once!"

"Good. Then there is another matter. You will divide some of your men into squads, and have them raid every fire house from the Battery to Forty-Second Street. They are to overpower the firemen—"

He paused as Nita suddenly called across the room from the radio: "Dick! Get this!"

She had caught the police short wave broadcast, and the headquarters voice was coming into the room:

"All cars converge on Chinatown! Report to Inspector Logan, who is searching for the Spider there. It is reported that the parties who participated in the raid on the building on the Drive were Chinese. Entire district is to be combed, and all known tong leaders are to be picked up. Wanted for questioning—"

Here followed a list of Chinese names, among which was that of Wang Chung!

Wentworth glanced at his Chinese host, who shrugged. "The police do not know of this retreat, Spider. They will go to my curio store on Pell Street, which is merely a blind. But Bart Peyton, of course, knows of this place, as does Tang-akhmut himself. If either of them should inform the police, we may expect a raid at any moment!"

Wentworth nodded. "We've got to evacuate."

"I have another place, Spider, which I hope is unknown to Tang-akhmut. We can reach it by an underground passage from the cellar of this house. Those are the sleeping quarters where my men rest when they are not working. We can retire there. If the police are very thorough, they may uncover that place, but—" he shrugged—"we must chance it."

"All right," said Wentworth. "Move the wounded there, and the women. Give me a car, so I can take Miss Grant to her father. If I can show him that his daughter is no longer in the power of Tang-akhmut, perhaps he'll call off his dogs. Give your men the instructions I have given you, as regards the raid on the Finney Finance Company."

Wang Chung smiled. "I will do better than that Spider. I will lead them myself. Your plan is dangerous. We may all die tonight. But I will put my trust in you."

"Thank you, Wang Chung. Let's hope that tonight's work will once and for all break the power of Tang-akhmut!"

CHAPTER 8
"HE IS MUCH BETTER DEAD!"

THE HOME of Acting Police Commissioner Darwin Grant was in one of those staid brownstone houses on

Lexington Avenue which are relics of a slower-moving and more stately society than that of today. Its austere front gave no hint of the agony of soul and mind that was being endured within.

The ground floor front room had been equipped as a combination office and sitting room, and it was from here that Grant ran the police department tonight. Almost every moment since his return, he had been on the telephone, issuing new orders for the concentration of men in the hunt for the Spider, in checking the disposition of those officers who had been detailed to guard the square block in which the Finney Finance Company was located. Then the new and startling attack on the building on the Drive had come in over the teletype and he had been busy issuing new orders.

His thin face was haggard, his mustache had lost its starch. He looked up petulantly as the uniformed policeman on duty in the hall entered to announce visitors. For a moment his face lighted up. He had remained carefully at home all evening, in the hope that the man he supposed to be Khandra Veg would come as promised, with news of Marcia. But his face grew sullen as the officer gave the men's names:

"Mr. Eustace Finney, and John Doane to see you, sir. They came separately, but Mr. Doane thinks you will not object to his presence while you talk to Mr. Finney. Mr. Doane is gathering material for his early morning broadcast, and Mr. Finney consented to his being present, if it's agreeable to you, sir."

Grant made a weary gesture with his hand. "All right, show them both in."

132

John Doane was the broadcaster who had earlier in the evening sounded the tentative note of sympathy—for the Spider. Eustace Finney was the head of the loan company which the Spider had pledged to rob tonight. Strange companions, thought Grant. He arose as the two men entered, shook hands with both. Finney was bald, sharp-nosed, thin-lipped, with an overbearing manner. Doane was tall, and carried himself with a good deal of poise. He spoke with restraint, in a voice so well modulated that it had become a favorite among news listeners in a short time. He apologized for intruding and glanced half humorously at Finney.

"Of course, it's quite sporting of Mr. Finney here to permit me to be present after the sympathetic way in which I spoke about the Spider tonight. But I can't help feeling that the man is not the criminal he is made out to be."

Finney motioned impatiently. "I don't care what you think of him, Doane, all I want is to be assured that he doesn't break into my vaults tonight." He pointed a finger at Grant. "Tell you what I want, Grant. Since hearing about that business up on the Drive, I've been thinking that maybe the Spider is smart enough to make good his boast about my vaults. So I sent an armored truck down there to take out certain papers that I wouldn't want to fall into his hands. But your men were all around, and they wouldn't even let the truck into the block. I don't care about the cash—we're insured. But I've got to get those papers out of there. Will you give me an order to your men?"

Grant shook his head in the negative. "Not tonight, Finney. Not a thing goes into that block till morning. And you don't have to worry. A mouse couldn't get in to the vaults. We've even got the cellars guarded!"

Finney's face was suddenly vindictive. He glanced sideways at Doane, then drew the acting commissioner to one side. He spoke very low, in a rasping whisper that grated on the official's ear. "Grant, you've got to get the Spider tonight. He slipped through your net at the bridge, and he got away up there on the Drive. If he succeeds in looting my vaults tonight, you will—regret it!"

Grant looked at him quizzically. "Regret it? How?

Finney dropped his voice even lower. "There is a certain mutual friend of ours—shall I name him? I believe—er—that your daughter has come under the influence of this mutual friend. That friend demands the capture of the Spider—if you ever want to see your daughter again!"

DARWIN GRANT'S face grew suddenly haggard. "My daughter! What do you know about her?" he demanded tautly. He had heard rumors through the city that the Finney Finance Company was only the mask for Tang-akhmut's financial operations. He had suspected as much, too, when the Spider announced that he was going to loot their vaults.

The company had sprung up like a mushroom in the last year or so, and they lent money in small sums to workingmen and poorly paid clerks, charging only a very low rate of interest. At first they had been hailed as a philanthropic institution. It was still so viewed by many. But reports had been coming in that those who borrowed were required to attend strange meetings, where queer things were done.

The police had not interfered, had not sought to check the credibility of these reports, for there was no charge against the company. And later, the powerful influence of Tang-akhmut had been exercised to keep the Finney Finance Company secure from investigation. Those who borrowed from it, and who might have been in the best position to relate what took place at those secret meetings, were remarkably close-mouthed. One or two had offered to make statements, but always some sad accident would happen to those, and their lips were sealed forever.

Now, Grant recalled all these rumors. Was Finney in league with Tang-akhmut? Of course he was; otherwise he would not know about Marcia. The acting commissioner gripped the financier's sleeve. "God, Finney, what do you know about my daughter? Is—is she well? I—I was hoping for news tonight—"

He paused, glancing over at John Doane, who was politely disinterested in the conversation, standing at the window and looking out into the street.

Suddenly, Doane seemed to tense at something he saw out there in front of the house. He raised the window to look out, and Grant rushed to his side.

"Marcia!" he exclaimed, pushing the other aside.

There, at the curb, was a sedan with a Chinese chauffeur. And alighting from the car was a man in a low-brimmed felt hat, who was helping a young woman out to the sidewalk. The young woman was Marcia Grant!

Darwin Grant was trembling as he leaned over the sill. Marcia looked up, started to wave. And just then, from both sides of the house, a swarm of small, wiry men dashed toward the car, knives gleaming in the air.

Grant shrieked: "No, no! Marcia!"

The man in the low-brimmed hat was quick to act. Almost before the first of the assailants had reached the car, he had pushed Marcia back into it, and two guns had appeared in his hands, blazing at the small attackers. Slashing bursts of fire darted from the twin muzzles of those guns, hurling the little men back upon each other. Guns barked in answer to his, and lead pinged against the windows and body of the sedan.

The man in the low-brimmed hat emptied his guns coolly, then whirled and darted into the sedan, which accelerated swiftly, and roared away from the curb. The little men disappeared into the night, leaving four dead on the sidewalk. Abruptly all was still again as the uniformed policeman came running from the house.

Grant was pounding his fists against the window sill in a frenzy of excitement. "Marcia!" he was shouting. "Marcia dear! O God, bring her back to me! He was bringing her to me! He was keeping his word!"

John Doane put a hand on his shoulder. "Take it easy, Commissioner. Your daughter wasn't hurt. Whoever that was with her, he can certainly fight. He got her away safely. But tell me, who was it that promised to bring her to you?"

Grant sank into a chair, his head in his hands. "It's no use, they won't let him bring her. They'll keep her away from me. I—I've got to do what they tell me!"

Doane glanced across Grant's shoulder to Finney, then

patted the distraught father on the back. "Maybe I can help you, Commissioner. If you'll tell me who it was that was bringing her back, maybe I can get in touch with him over the radio. I could tell him to communicate with me—"

GRANT LOOKED up, suddenly hopeful. "You could do that? I'd never thank you enough. That was Khandra Veg, a servant of The Man from the East—the one who is so mysterious."

He swung on John Doane. "You want to have a scoop for your broadcast, Doane? You want to give them real news? Well, I'm going to crack this thing wide open! Tang-akhmut has been holding my daughter, and so making me allow him a free hand to organize the biggest crime combine in the city. He gets dupes to kill and rob for him, and I have to keep my men off the trail, for fear of what will happen to my daughter—"

His voice was interrupted by the single low *pop* of a silenced gun. A curl of smoke twisted from the muzzle of the pistol in Eustace Finney's hand. Finney watched impassively while Grant dropped to the floor, with a hole in the back of his head. Then he raised his eyes and looked at John Doane.

"The man talked too much," he said softly. "He is much better dead!"

Just then the door was shoved open, and the uniformed patrolman burst in, gun in hand, breathless from his run to the street. "Commissioner!" he gasped. "It was—"

He stopped short, staring at Finney, at the still smoking gun, at the dead body of Grant. Finney's lips twisted, and he raised the gun again. The policeman fired at the same moment that

Finney did. The cop was smashed back against the door, a slug in his heart. Finney fell forward. A big black splotch, like a third eye, appeared in his forehead.

The room was still filled with the deafening explosion of the dead cop's gun, as John Doane left the dead lying where they were, and passed quickly out of the room, into the street....

CHAPTER 9
THE TITANS MEET

T HE FINNEY FINANCE COMPANY occupied the entire six floors of the Finney Building, on Fourteenth Street between Union Square and Seventh Avenue. The ground floor was taken up by an immense, bank-like office, fronted with plate glass windows. A large poster in the window announced:

"Loans from twenty-five to two hundred dollars can be secured without delay, and without red tape or co-makers!"

Tonight, however, there was no business. But the Finney Building was ablaze with light. Incandescents glowed on every floor, and police with sub-machine guns could be seen through the plate glass windows of the store front, waiting tensely for the promised arrival of the Spider.

Crowds of curious people, attracted by the deadline which the police had drawn around the block, thronged the sidewalks of the opposite sides of the streets, moving on surlily and reluctantly when ordered by the reserves stationed there. Among these crowds, a close observer might have noted that there was an unusually large proportion of Chinese.

The yellow men were as inconspicuous as they could make themselves, being attired in conventional Western fashion. But there were suspicious bulges under the armpits of all these slant-eyed, hard-bitten Chinese; and strangely enough, each of these men seemed to gravitate at one time or another toward a spot in the park, where stood a single man.

THIS MAN kept his eyes constantly on the ground, and his face was effectively hidden from passers-by. The policemen patrolling the park did not think of looking here for one who was on the wanted list. But had they accosted him, they would have recognized him at once as Wang Chung, whose name had been broadcast over the police radio only a little while earlier as a suspect in the raid on the Drive. Each of the Chinese who passed him, stopped for only a second, and whispered to him. And Wang Chung swiftly replied, sending them to take stations at various spots in the street, giving them hasty directions.

"At the signal," he told each of them, "you will do what you have been told to do. But bear in mind that there is to be no killing. That is the demand of the queer white man whom we help tonight!"

Wang Chung, after the last of his men had received instructions and had drifted away, glanced about anxiously, as if awaiting the arrival of someone else. Time drifted on. It was two o'clock in the morning.

Still the Spider had not struck. Many of the curiosity-seekers began to grow sleepy, to leave the scene. The crowds became less thick. But the Chinese remained.

Across the street, on Broadway, the hatchet man, Lee, came

out of the phone booth in a restaurant, where he had been waiting for a call for the last hour. He hurried across the park to Wang Chung, spoke excitedly in Cantonese:

"All is ready, Wang Chung. The Spider has just given the word."

Wang Chung nodded jerkily. He seemed to share the excitement of his lieutenant. He turned, facing north, and raised his arm straight up in the air. In a building on the northwest corner of Fifteenth Street, opposite the blockaded block, and in a building on the southwest corner of Fourteenth Street, almost diagonally opposite the Finney Building, two Chinese with spy glasses had been watching Wang Chung closely.

Now, as he raised his arm, they put down the spy glasses and hurriedly moved about the rooms where they had been watching. In a few moments, dense clouds of smoke began to emanate from the windows of those buildings. Tongues of flame licked forth with the smoke. Simultaneously, further down the block, on both Fourteenth and Fifteenth, other buildings began to vomit flame and smoke.

The Chinese in the street began to shout, and to point at those thick billowing clouds of smoke, crying: "Fieh! Fieh! Big fieh!"

The police stared up at the flames suspiciously. This then, was the way of the Spider's attack. They tightened their grips on their guns, refused grimly to be lured into leaving their posts. Inspector Thomas, in charge of all the police forces in the area, who was giving orders from a squad car on Fourteenth Street, sent a man to ring in the fire alarm, while at the same time the men on Fifteenth Street sent in an alarm of their own.

In a surprisingly short time, fire engines began to clang into the streets. Inexplicably, the lights in Union Square, in Fourteenth and Fifteenth Streets, went out. The area was thrown into pitch blackness, except for the occasional tongue of flame that licked from the windows of the burning structures. The police watched tensely, ready for anything, but no overt move was made.

THICK, ACRID smoke began to come from the buildings, stinging the eyes of the police, cutting at their throats, driving them back. Inspector Thomas looked around desperately for the fire commissioner, who should be here at a time like this, but could not find him. Instead, he approached a red fire chief's car, shouted at the uniformed man in it:

"What'll we do? We can't stay here! That smoke's too much for us!"

All the firemen had donned gas masks now, and they were cluttering the street with ladders and hose. The big spotlights of the engines were focused on the various buildings, affording the only light in the street. The fire chief got out of the car, shouted to Inspector Thomas: "I think that's some sort of gas. You better clear out of the street. It might be deadly."

Inspector Thomas protested. "But we can't drop the guard on the Finney Company. This was done by the Spider, I bet. He wants to get us out of here!"

The fire chief shrugged. "Suit yourself. If you want to take a chance, go ahead and stay. I'm telling you that you and your men will all be candidates for the hospital!"

Thomas cursed, and ran back to his car. He issued orders to

his men to move into the Finney Building. The gas fumes should not be able to reach them there. But even as he spoke, a number of black objects with remarkable accuracy were hurled from the buildings across the street. The objects shattered the windows of the Finney Building, and exploded within, sending forth thick jets of smoke that bit into the lungs of the police.

Thomas threw out more orders: "Fight your way into the buildings, boy—"

He was interrupted by the fire chief he had just spoken to, who came running over with a gas mask on his face. The fire chief raised his mask long enough to shout:

"Get your men out of here quick, Inspector, or they'll all keel over. And clear them out of the Finney Building. We've got to go in there!"

"But damn it, man, the vaults! We can't leave the vaults unguarded!"

The fire chief grunted. "You don't have to worry. The Spider can't get in there any more than you can. And my own men will take good care of the vaults—very good care!" he added under his breath.

Reluctantly, Thomas gasped out the necessary orders, through lungs that were already gasping, and the police retired to Union Square.

The fire fighters, in their gas masks, dragged hoses into the Finney Building, but queerly, did not attempt to put out the fire.

The fire chief issued them orders—not in English, but in Cantonese! And they hurried down toward the vaults. There several of them, acting as if they had rehearsed this portion of the task, laid sticks of dynamite against the huge doors, ran out into the street. In a moment there was a tremendous concussion, and the whole building shook.

The next instant, the firemen were racing back through the smoke of the explosion, flashlights in their hands. The vault door had practically disintegrated under the explosion, and the vaults of the Finney Finance Company lay open. The firemen hurried inside, under the directions of the fire chief, and picked up stacks of currency which they carried out to the engines. Trip after trip they made, emptying the vaults in a few minutes.

The fire chief himself was poking around in the inner recesses of the vaults, and suddenly he uttered an exclamation of satisfaction, as he found a stack of loose-leaf books, and several packages of envelopes. He glanced hurriedly through them, found that they contained the names of Peyton and many other men. These, too, he ordered his men to carry up. Within twelve minutes of the arrival of the engines, the vaults had been emptied. Outside, flame and smoke was still spouting from windows all along the block, as well as from the Finney Building, but queerly, though the firemen were making no real effort to fight the fires, they were not spreading!

At the end of the street, where the police were clustered thickly about the car of Inspector Thomas, one of the officers returned from the telephone to salute and report:

"I phoned Commissioner Grant, as you ordered, sir, to report developments. And—and—they tell me, sir, that he—he's been killed!"

Thomas edged forward in his seat. "*Killed!* Good God—"

HE STOPPED as a man pushed his way through the press of uniformed and plain clothes police, to the side of the car. The man was John Doane, the radio announcer. And for one who was interested in events merely for their news value, he seemed strangely perturbed.

The short wave radio on the dashboard suddenly sprang to life, and the headquarters broadcaster's voice blared into the air:

"Special emergency notice. All police, beware of bogus firemen. Seize all fire apparatus met in the streets, and arrest the crews. We have just learned that all fire houses south of Fifty-Ninth Street were raided by Chinese, and the firemen overpowered! Inspector Thomas! Do not allow bogus fire companies access to the Finney Building—"

Thomas ripped out an oath, started to get out of the car. But John Doane suddenly screamed;

"Damn him! Damn him! He's beaten me!" Doane's eyes were abruptly burning with a strange light.

Inspector Thomas seized his arm. "What's the matter with you, Doane? What do you mean? What have you got to do with this?"

"You fool!" screamed Doane. "You think I am merely a radio announcer?" He drew himself up. "I am also Tang-akhmut, the Living Pharaoh! I am the man who controls this city! I am the man whose orders you have been obeying. Come quickly, before the Spider empties my vaults!"

He turned and ran into the darkness of Fourteenth Street. Thomas grimaced to his subordinates. "My God, why do we have to take orders from that scum? I'd rather work with the Spider!"

A police lieutenant growled: "What do you know! That guy has been snooping around, hearing us talk, getting the low-down on a lot of stuff, and all the time we thought he was only a radio announcer!" He shrugged. "We better follow him, if we want to keep our jobs!"

But Tang-akhmut had already disappeared in the turmoil of the fire-lit street. In the darkness he coughed as the smoke fumes hit him, and he drew a gun. Behind him, the police advanced cautiously. Tang-akhmut heard the motors of fire trucks starting, and he knew that the work of the bogus firemen was finished. Madly, he clutched at the sleeve of a gas-masked fire chief who was hurrying past him. The fire chief swung on him, stared through the gas mask at him. Tang-akhmut reached out swiftly and tore the mask from the man's face. For a long moment the two men stood stock still and looked into each other's eyes.

The Spider said quietly: "I was hoping you'd come, Tang-akhmut!"

THE MAN who claimed to be the Living Pharaoh snarled his hate, and raised his gun.

As his finger pressed on the trigger, the Spider struck his hand aside with a swift motion. The gun exploded in the air. The Spider bored in, pistoning blows at Tang-akhmut, sending him reeling, off balance. Wentworth's eyes were gleaming with victory.

The one thing he had hoped for had come to pass. He could throw Tang-akhmut into one of the fire trucks, carry him off. Now was his chance! He sent a hard right to Tang-akhmut's jaw, and the Living Pharaoh slumped on his knees. The Spider

145

stepped in to follow him up, when an avalanche of police smashed into them.

Thomas was leading his men back into the street, with drawn guns. Smoke or no smoke, they were going to shoot down the bogus firemen. And the Spider was hurled back from his prey, forced to twist and dodge to escape the hail of lead the police sent at him in the dark.

He left Tang-akhmut lying in the street, ran swiftly to the curb, zigzagging to escape the whining slugs. The Chinese pseudo-firemen, still in their gas masks, had turned off all but one hose. The Spider seized this last remaining hose and heaved it around so that it jetted its thick, powerful stream directly at the advancing police. They were bowled over like ninepins, sent floundering in the gutter. He continued to play it on the police, preventing them from getting to their feet, while the others quickly got the engines in motion.

With a dangerous clamor of bells and sirens, the fire trucks sped down the street toward Seventh Avenue. The Spider dropped the hose, leaped into the fire chief's car, and followed the last of them, driving through the wide lane which the crowd opened for the clanging juggernauts.

From here on, the operation would be simple. The cash removed from the Finney vaults amounted, at a rough estimate, to millions. Much of this was money that had been stripped from Wentworth by Tang-akhmut not so long ago. And it was with Wentworth's money that Tang-akhmut had been making the loans that had brought him recruits throughout the city. Now, that money was recovered. With it, Wentworth had the papers which had enforced Tang-akhmut's power over so many people; so that the man's vast influence over the people of the city would be forever broken.

Along the river front, fast launches were waiting to tranship the money and the records to the *Orient Queen,* where they would be out of the reach of the police and of The Man from the East.

But Wentworth, as he drove behind the long fleet of fire trucks, felt no elation, only a great weariness and depression of spirit. For though he had beaten off the vicious attempt of Tang-akhmut to enslave the city, he knew that the Living Pharaoh was still alive, that he would never rest in the mad struggle for power. Tang-akhmut would be back. The man's resources were apparently limitless. He would be back—more deadly, more vicious than ever.

Richard Wentworth's lips tightened as he gripped the steering wheel of the car. He had snatched victory out of the jaws of circumstance. Men like Bart Peyton, and others whose records were no longer in the hands of Tang-akhmut, need fear the Egyptian no more. They would not pillage and loot at his command. For the time being the city could breath easy, work back into its normal stride.

But in the meantime, the Spider must prepare for the inevitable return of The Man from the East! A harsh laugh floated from his lips.

The Spider would be ready!

POPULAR HERO PULPS AVAILABLE NOW:

THE SECRET 6

- ❑ #1: The Red Shadow — $13.95
- ❑ #2: House of Walking Corpses — $13.95
- ❑ #3: The Monster Murders — $13.95
- ❑ #4: The Golden Alligator — $13.95

OPERATOR 5

- ❑ #1: The Masked Invasion — $13.95
- ❑ #2: The Invisible Empire — $13.95
- ❑ #3: The Yellow Scourge — $13.95
- ❑ #4: The Melting Death — $13.95
- ❑ #5: Cavern of the Damned — $13.95
- ❑ #6: Master of Broken Men — $13.95
- ❑ #7: Invasion of the Dark Legions — $13.95
- ❑ #8: The Green Death Mists — $13.95
- ❑ #9: Legions of Starvation — $13.95
- ❑ #10: The Red Invader — $13.95
- ❑ #11: The League of War-Monsters — $13.95
- ❑ #12: The Army of the Dead — $13.95
- ❑ #13: March of the Flame Marauders — $13.95
- ❑ #14: Blood Reign of the Dictator — $13.95
- ❑ #15: Invasion of the Yellow Warlords — $13.95
- ❑ #16: Legions of the Death Master — $13.95
- ❑ #17: Hosts of the Flaming Death — $13.95
- ❑ #18: Invasion of the Crimson Death Cult — $13.95
- ❑ #19: Attack of the Blizzard Men — $13.95
- ❑ #20: Scourge of the Invisible Death — $13.95

DUSTY AYRES AND HIS BATTLE BIRDS

- ❑ #1: Black Lightning! — $13.95
- ❑ #2: Crimson Doom — $13.95
- ❑ #3: The Purple Tornado — $13.95
- ❑ #4: The Screaming Eye — $13.95
- ❑ #5: The Green Thunderbolt — $13.95
- ❑ #6: The Red Destroyer — $13.95
- ❑ #7: The White Death — $13.95
- ❑ #8: The Black Avenger — $13.95
- ❑ #9: The Silver Typhoon — $13.95
- ❑ #10: The Troposphere F-S — $13.95
- ❑ #11: The Blue Cyclone — $13.95
- ❑ #12: The Tesla Raiders — $13.95

MAVERICKS

- ❑ #1: Five Against the Law — $12.95
- ❑ #2: Mesquite Manhunters — $12.95
- ❑ #3: Bait for the Lobo Pack — $12.95
- ❑ #4: Doc Grimson's Outlaw Posse — $12.95
- ❑ #5: Charlie Parr's Gunsmoke Cure — $12.95

THE MYSTERIOUS WU FANG

- ❑ #1: The Case of the Six Coffins — $12.95
- ❑ #2: The Case of the Scarlet Feather — $12.95
- ❑ #3: The Case of the Yellow Mask — $12.95
- ❑ #4: The Case of the Suicide Tomb — $12.95
- ❑ #5: The Case of the Green Death — $12.95
- ❑ #6: The Case of the Black Lotus — $12.95
- ❑ #7: The Case of the Hidden Scourge — $12.95

www.ingramcontent.com/pod-product-compliance
Lightning Source LLC
Chambersburg PA
CBHW020136180626
46810CB00004B/1585